TROLL

A very old story...
By Richard Sutton

Discover other titles by Richard Sutton
at Amazon, Barnes & Noble, or Smashwords in all
eBook formats and at a bookstore near you:

The Red Gate

The Gatekeepers

Home

Visit the author's blog and news site:
www.sailletales.com to see what's coming…

Author's Typographical Note: This book is set in Times Roman for clarity and ease of reading. The ragged right margin was chosen specifically as it is known in design circles, to ease eye strain. When blocks of text contain the variable white word spacing found in justified margins (left and right) these gaps effectively become visual rivers of white on the page. The use of justified margins is an artifact of hot metal typography loaded into galley frames for printing. It is not necessary in today's technology, so I have made the decision to make my books readable, first. I hope my readers will appreciate this decision.

The following is a work of fiction. Any similarity to locations or people alive or dead or forgotten, is strictly coincidence and purely unintentional.

\# \# \# \#

A High Valley in Norway. Present Day.

It had been a long, difficult excavation. The removal of the rubble blocking the entrance had progressed much too slowly; and without any real value to what they had found inside, so far, many were losing their faith that their time had not been wasted. When Jen's team had sent word that they had found something they couldn't explain, it sparked hope again.

The last of the dusty excavation assistants squeezed into the narrow space remaining within the inner cave. The motion sent another blast of sooty smoke swirling among the already gathered group. Their sense of anxious anticipation was as pervasive as the sting of the smoke and the musty air. Their dig leader pushed into the waiting crowd.

"It's the smoke from the torches – it's making my eyes water… gimme a minute."

"The electrics are getting pretty dim. Sorry about the smoke."

Dr. Ariel Connor wrung the sweat from the bandana that had been keeping her hair off her forehead and wiped her face, then her eyes, gently, to remove some of the grime. She was running out of steam. She crawled up closer to where the light was throwing shadows on the stone wall. A protruding rock, jutting from the cave floor poked her shin as she settled down on her hands and knees.

"Shit! OK, Jens – I can see now. What did you find back here?"

Jens Eriksson, the excavation manager held his torch up to shine as much light as he could on the cleft in the cave's face. Two burly, dig assistants from the University were sweeping away grime and dirt with short brushes. "Ariel, can you see that, alright?"

"Yes. It's…" she hesitated, then reached out to lightly touch the dressed stone surface that extended out from the narrow fissure. "It's carved, not a natural formation. There is… color beneath the carbonate crust, along with tool markings."

"That's what I got, too. Do you agree about it being pigmented – painted?"

"She brought her own torch closer to the surface. "Yes, a red pigment. It follows down the fissure, here." She motioned for Jens' torch to be brought lower as well. When it was descending towards the cleft, she raised her hand.

"Look – it's darker at the bottom of the cleft."

"Yes. I see that. It's a pretty good likeness, isn't it?"

Ariel, now on her hands and knees next to the rock wall, grinned. She moved back for a better view of the surface carving.

"Amazing." She nodded her head, adding "It really confirms some of what I've been thinking, you know?" She motioned again for the light and pointed to the widest spot in the fissure, where the black depths within swallowed the light the torch could provide. "…but we'll know more once we get inside."

Jens agreed, but rubbing his chin replied, "That's sure, but who could possibly fit?"

Ariel stood, brushing off her khakis. "A child will fit. How appropriate, don't you think?"

# # # #

Closer to the cave's mouth and many thousands of years before Dr. Connor's team broke through the rubble that had blocked its entrance for centuries, Mokolo stirred in his sleep. He slowly woke to the comforting smell of the fire. It had been a hard, restless night and the morning sun had not yet broken through the crags at the east of the valley. Night still lay thick everywhere.

Mokolo dreamed he'd felt his father's hand on his shoulder, but he was mistaken. He blinked his dark, deep-set eyes, rubbing them to wipe off the sleep sand and then sat up. Looking out past the cave's mouth to the river, far below, he could just make it out as a faint silver ribbon running through the darkness.

His shoulder still ached from the fall two days earlier, and he was massaging it when a light touch upon his hand brought his attention back to the morning's work. He looked up into the stern face of the Chief of the Hunt, Datolo, who stood motioning to him, in the firelight, to join other men he could see already gathered further back, near the sputtering fire.

"Mokolo, you must help us make ready!" the Chief hissed at him, his stern eyes blazing from under bold, dark eyebrows, "We're away before first light!"

He nodded, touching Datolo's hard hand to reassure him that he'd be up with them. The hunt day had been set, but had been postponed because of the loss of Mokolo's father, Slatolo. It was a terrible pain in his heart, tearing at him, but he rose from his pine-bough and bearskin bed and joined other men to prepare for the hunt as he had done so many times since becoming a man, some two winters before. As he rose, he thought of his journey to man-hood, and how his father's death had disturbed his sense of accomplishment and his sense of purpose.

Though the cave was still dark, firelight danced off the near walls, highlighting some still-sleeping forms, bundled against the early fall chill. The sentries' beds had been cleared from the cave mouth, back against the walls and at the fire; the hunters were rubbing their spear points sharp against stones that held the fire's warmth. As he approached the group, the smoke burned his eyes in the familiar, comforting way it always had. He found a place

near his friend, Baaktolo and began heating the point of
one of the new long spears over the flames. Gathered
nearby were the two- hands-plus-four that he'd been
preparing. Recently completed, each of them would be
carried along on the hunt, even if he must remain behind.
At least his work would do something for the clan.

There was no speaking, for fear of waking those who
slept further back in the cave, but as he watched the tip
grow hot and begin to smoke, Mokolo could see the
twinkling eyes of a few small boys huddled further back
in the dark cave to watch the hunters leave. Every small
face he saw resembled his own. They were all family.
Connected. He remembered many such mornings when he
was a boy, watching his father join the hunters before the
sun returned. It had been very exciting to him then, and he
mused to himself how the reality of going out on the hunt
before the sun seemed just hard work now.

Withdrawing his spear, the still smoking point was
rubbed back and forth through a notch in the nearest
stone, polishing and hardening it. A small piece of dried
meat was passed to him, and he accepted it gratefully, its
hard surface becoming savory as he chewed it. Mokolo's
stomach sent up a rumble to let him know it was also
grateful for the small meal. His friend Baaktolo laid his
hand upon Mokolo's shoulder and rose from the fire, one
more spear ready for the hunt.

The Water Mother, old Kin'kala carefully filled each
hunter's water gourd from her large, pitch-lined water
basket as they stood waiting at the fireside. Soon all
hunters were ready to leave. There were two-hands-plus-
three of them, including the Chief of the Hunt and they
grasped each other's wrists around the fire, making a
connected circle. The Water Mother withdrew into the
shadows away from the firelight as Datolo spoke quietly.

His broad mouth revealing the trace of a smile, he
offered a prayer. "May our Great Mother and our Lesser

Mothers all bless us in this Hunt and bring even the fast running fourlegs to us easily! May our steps be light and silent and our spears sharp and true!" The gathered hunters all responded by clapping both hands flat upon their own chests in unison, the muffled thump echoing slightly along the back of the cave and signaling to those remaining in the darkness that the hunters were leaving. None of the hunters turned to look behind them as they strode out of the cave mouth, led by their chief. Their soft footfalls were the only sound as they filed down the high pathway and out towards the ledge.

Inside, the Water Mother returned her water basket to its place, near the wall on the fire's left side, then turned toward the deeper darkness where her soft bed waited. It was good, she thought to herself, to be older, to be able to serve the rest, but also to get back into bed on a chilly morning instead of stumbling down the rocky path towards the valley floor. She passed the old Fire Master, Tik'olo, who was dragging two logs towards the rear of the fire pit to warm the cave for the day. His two young fire helpers struggled with their additional bundles of twigs and bark. Mokolo noticed and ran over to help them before they dropped the loads in a clatter. Their soft morning chatter echoed off the deeper walls behind them, still in shadow.

Light began painting the closest treetops with a pink glow. The young boys remained at their stations near the fire, watching the light return to the valley. As the sun finally made its way over the Eastern crags at the narrows, spilling warm light into the cave's mouth, the boys heard the Mother's morning song begin from behind them in the darkness. Its soft, reassuring melody resounded off the walls filling both boys with a sense of peaceful happiness. The day had returned, and soon the women – the Lesser Mothers – would begin appearing to greet the day at the cave's mouth with their offerings of a pinch of pollen, tossed into the morning air.

The hunters made their way below, as silently as they could, and the new day began for the Valley People as it had for many generations before them. The Fire Master's young assistants carefully tended the fire and watched darkness flee the Valley, trailing the blue curtain of sky behind it. In exactly the same way, other boys like them had done as far back as memory could travel.

Chapter 2

After the hunters had departed, women appeared in small, sleepy groups of two or three, making their morning prayers at the cave mouth, then returning to the tasks awaiting them back in their deeper section of the cave. The faint cry of a baby could be heard now and again, calling to its Lesser Mother until she returned to raise it up, kiss its little face, and give it the breast it cried for. Whenever they heard the cries suddenly stop, the boys smiled, remembering their own Lesser Mothers' comforting care.

One boy's stomach rumbled and he laughed, poking the other with a stick. The other's stomach also rumbled, and they both turned their eyes back into the cave, where the Food Mother and her young helpers were approaching with their baskets.

The older woman carried a large, tightly woven basket that had several other men of diminishing size resting within. As she approached the fire, the two fire tenders withdrew respectfully, lowering their eyes as they returned to the nearest wall. The Food Mother's helpers, set their baskets of nuts and acorn flour down upon the largest hearthstone, along with a bundle of dried meat rolled in skins. They stayed close by the older woman, but would occasionally steal glances at the boys at the cave wall, who were also stealing glances at the girls, whenever the Food Mother's back was turned. It was a great game, and very entertaining for the boys, who of course, slept and stayed with the men. This small interchange was their closest contact with the young girls and women, except their own mother men, whom they were allowed to approach directly.

The Food Mother handed a large water gourd to her nearest assistant, who headed for the water basket on her side of the cave. That was also where the two fire tenders sat. A sharp word from The Food Mother, who would not tolerate such foolishness, sent them both scurrying over to the other side of the cave so the girl could get cooking water safely. The girl glanced at the last one to leave just as he glanced at her, and their eyes met.

Both children were frightened by the implications of clear sight into another's eyes. Both turned away quickly, breaking the stares. They would have to speak with their elders later, to ask if they had made sin or trouble for their clan. The girl, dipping the large gourd into the Water Master's basket, shook her head slowly, from side to side almost as if she were trying to deny what had just happened.

As she returned with the full gourd, she looked into the Food Mother's face expecting a rebuke, but none came. It remained her secret. The old woman took the large gourd, pouring its contents into the largest basket and returning it to the girl for another filling. While she was filling the gourd twice more, the other girl was slowly stirring the acorn meal and nuts into the basket as more water was added.

When three gourds of water had been stirred together with the mixture, the Food Mother began tearing small strips of the dried meat from the bundle and placing them into the mush. She then drew two hot stones from within the fire, using green willow forks and carefully placed them right into the mush in the basket, one by one. Both girls watched this tricky operation closely. Someday soon, each of them would have to duplicate this important step without being burned or dropping the stones into the basket too quickly. Food, as they had been taught, was much too precious to waste or damage through poor cooking habits. Soon, the mush was bubbling away, sending its savory scent throughout the cave.

The Food Mother began her Eating Song, which, with its quick, happy melody, brought the rest of the clan out from the deeper parts of the cave. They each held their own eating gourds before them, in line, awaiting their turn as the Food Mother's song ended. The remaining boys, Mokolo and the other makers and the two older men along with the day's sentries stood aside, their eyes downcast waiting for the women to receive their food and withdraw. After the last girl had returned to her place in the recesses of the cave, they formed a line, and each held his gourd up to the Food Mother, eyes still downcast, thanking her in turn and withdrawing to their own places, near the cave's mouth.

As they began eating from their gourds using their fingers, they began a cheerful conversation about the prospects for the days hunt. Mokolo began, his eyes straining out over the Valley, to catch sight of the hunters "Do you think they've reached the river yet?" he asked his friend.

Baaktolo looked out over the ledge outside the cave's mouth. Shaking his head, he replied "No, not yet" as he slurped his fingers clean. He added "Remember the fourlegs we saw before..." his speech stopped, and he looked at Mokolo, hoping his friend understood. It would not do well to mention those who were gone from life. It would bring trouble to the hunt, so he waited until Mokolo nodded, then continued, "...close enough to hit with a rock from here!"

Mokolo laughed and added, in an exaggerated voice, "maybe if you were much bigger and much stronger!" His friend gave him a shove, and they both laughed.

One of the sentries added his take on the hunt, adding "It's a good thing our hunters don't rely upon the wisdom of such as you two, or we'd never get any meat at all!" The sentry turned to his watch mate and they spoke quietly about hunts still in memory.

"I'm glad I'm here today," the sentry said finally, patting his ample belly. "I'm not happy chewing only a tiny bit of dried meat to start my day, are you?"

The sentry's friend replied "Next week, it'll be your turn in the hunt and that's all you'll get, so enjoy the remaining mornings while you can!" The sentry nodded and fell silent.

This was the Way of the Clan: all men that were able, added their strength and help to the weekly hunt. Men who were injured or ill, of course, were not expected to hunt, which is why Mokolo was able to spend his day making spears rather than crawling all over the valley floor with the rest. His friend, Baaktolo had been a hunter, too, until it became known that his hearing was afflicted. Men whose hearing or sight were afflicted or were lame or damaged were taught to be makers.

Baaktolo's days were spent making food and water gourds, crafting implements or weapons as needed by the clan. He especially was skilled at scratching beautiful, mystical shapes of four legged ones upon food gourds, and of the swimming ones upon the water gourds, along with tiny, cross-hatched or striped decorations. Each one he made was different, and its new owner was always pleased with his work. He was secretly happy that Mokolo had hurt his shoulder, as it gave him a companion while it healed. Of course, he didn't wish his friend any trouble and put that silly thought away. He hoped his companionship would help Mokolo through this hard time. Mokolo no longer had the guidance and help of his father. All Mokolo's clan brothers would have to take the place of his father and give him their help to guide him back into full manhood. Baaktolo would make sure in every way he could, that Mokolo's grief could be borne and though he would miss his companionship, Mokolo could return to himself.

After all had eaten, near the fire, the Food Mother meticulously cleaned the last of the warm mush from the stones and the inside of the cooking basket. She used a small, flat stick, wiping off each small bit into her own food gourd. As always, it was her lot to wait until all were fed before she ate and she made sure not a speck of food was ever wasted. It had been her Lesser Mother's job before her, and would be her own daughter's job when she had passed from them.

Her two helpers watched with care, to see how she found every tiny bit of food. They had already gathered their baskets and bundles, and waited for the Food Mother to finish her meal so that they might all return to the safety of the inner cave. On days of the hunt, it was quiet in the cave, only the voices of the other women and girls were heard, as the remaining men were busy with their work. But there was a great deal to do inside; there were the lessons and prayers must be made to the Great Mother and to their enemies, the powerful bears and the sharp toothed cats. Keeping them all safe took a great deal of time and effort. It was just as difficult as the hunter's work, and as the Food Mother finished, the two girls slowly stood, gathered their burdens and returned with her, to the inner cave, where their important work was beginning in earnest.

Chapter 3

Mokolo sat in his favorite spot just outside the cave's mouth, upon a large rock. The sun's light had bathed him in warmth for the past several hours, as he scraped new spears clean, from the saplings he'd piled up nearby. He was glad to have this work. It made him pay close attention to what he was doing so it would help keep his mind from wandering. Holding a sharpened flaked stone in a piece of skin in one hand, he drew it carefully, edge against the sapling and down, to remove the bark and any burrs or splinters that might remain. Leaving them would be a potential bit of trouble for a hunter, who needed all his attention on the hunt, and not on a hand hurt by an indifferent spear maker.

With each scraped stroke, the focus of his attention almost took away the image of his father's death. There had been many wounds. So many and a great deal of blood. Each wound had been made by the little feathered spears sent by their new enemies, the unknown other men who had just come into the valley. It had happened only two hand's days ago, and the memory, pain and resulting fear still was alive and fresh in his mind. He scraped harder, hoping to dispel the memory, but it did only a little good. He saw his father's face when he closed his eyes. So still… his bloody lips drawn back, his teeth clenched. His death had been painful, and from the marks on his neck, he'd struggled for a long time before he bled away his life.

Finished with one, Mokolo stood, and took up a new sapling. Each was cut to the same length as a man, and carefully sharpened into a point at one end. The other end was cut with a carefully measured notch and a rounded butt. The notch would fit into a spear throwing stick, giving much more power and distance than the spear in the hand alone. He proudly peeled away the bark nearest

the cleanly cut notch, and considered the fit. It would be
very good, secure and would let go at just the right angle
and amount of force. The thought made him shudder as
the memory of his father's dead body filled his thoughts
again. It was useless to resist it. The full memory of that
hunt crept back to him.

The hunt had gone well at first, as a large clan of the
fourlegs was seen and followed, silently and unseen. The
fourlegs were grazing along the other side of the river, and
moving toward the crags at the East end of the Valley.
They stalked them carefully through the first day and the
following day, but as the sun rose on the third day,
something must have spooked the fourlegs, since the clan
had moved quickly in the night. Two scouts were sent to
follow the trail, which seemed to lead close to the crags.

It made Mokolo very wary as he watched the scouts
disappear over the rise leading away from them and on
towards the crags. His father was one of the scouts. He
was always chosen because his skills at following a fast-
running four leg were unsurpassed among the hunters.
Mokolo was proud that his father could boast he was able
to get close enough to the fourlegs that he didn't even need
to throw his spear. He took them with knife alone!
Mokolo wanted to learn to be as skillful a hunter as his
father, so he was unhappy that he hadn't been chosen to
accompany him in finding where the four leg clan had
gone.

But stronger still, was his wariness that the trail
seemed to lead towards the crags at the narrow gorge.
Their enemies, the bears lived at the crags, and no one
wanted to go too near. The bears were a small clan, but
they were twice the height of a man, very fast, and very
strong, and could easily outrun and kill any hunter who
ventured into their part of the valley. In the old days, the
stories told of how the bears would come at night and
steal children, even women. They would never be seen

again, but it had been years since they had ventured up the Valley to the cave. There were very old stories, learned in the lessons that told of the clan's coming to the Valley, and fighting the bears with fire, to take the cave away from them. Since that time, the two clans were enemies and for many years, both the People and the bears knew the loss of death. Mokolo remembered how his father had killed two of them, and made their skins into beds for himself and Mokolo's mother. But not ever again. Mokolo wiped a tear from his eyes as the sad memory took hold. He thought again, of his father's last day.

The scouts had left to follow the fourlegs, but were not back by nightfall. Another man was chosen from among the hunters to climb a tree to see if a fire's light could be spotted from up in its branches, and sure enough, he saw fire -- but he saw two fires. Two fires. The hunters had argued about what that meant. Mokolo had listened as one said it meant the two scouts had fought and were keeping separate fires, but the Hunt Chief told him "Nonsense! No one would spend the night alone in the Valley by their own choice."

Other men wondered if the bear clan was also hunting, and wondered if they kept fires, too. There were many ideas, but none made any sense. In the end, Datolo, the Hunt Chief, only said, "We will wait for the light."

The next day, the hunters carefully crept out along the path the scouts had taken and by the time the sun had risen above their heads, they met one scout returning, on the run. Mokolo's father was not with him. He was covered with mud, and there were also some wounds and blood. One of his arms had what seemed to be a small broken spear protruding from beneath a wrapping of grass, mud and bark. When it had been cleaned, and his fear and weakness had left him, he was questioned.

"We never found the fourlegs" he said, but added, "Neither did we see bears. We followed the trail until the sun had lowered a bit and the fourlegs trail had again turned away from the crags, back towards the river, into the high grasses." He paused, as the fear in his memory returned for a moment.

"But what of Slatolo?" the chief asked him.

"Slatolo was in the grass ahead of me. He turned to tell me he was having trouble finding the trail, when there was a loud, sudden shout of a man's voice, then other men." He continued, "we shouted back, but the other men's cries were not understandable, and they were drawing nearer. We turned to run back into the forest to hide ourselves, but as we ran, small feathered spears began falling around us. I felt one enter my arm, and turned to see if Slatolo was following, just as he screamed. One of the small spears had struck him in the neck. Another had struck him in the back, and another had struck him in his shoulder. He fell on the ground within the tall grass, and blood flowed from his lips. I turned and ran up along the edge of the grass until I came to the edge of the trees. I took shelter and hid in the heavy brush."

His breath was coming in gasps, and the Hunt Chief laid his hand upon the stricken scout to calm him. The jagged wound in his upper arm was bound with grass and mud, but it still gave him a great deal of pain. His eyes darted from face to face, fearfully. He soon added, "I never returned to find Slatolo. I am sorry – I'm a coward!" he began to sob.

The chief turned to the hunters, including Mokolo, now very fearful, and with tears on his own cheeks, said, "The hunt is finished. We will return tomorrow to where Slatolo lies still, and we will bring him back to his home"

They watched again for fire from the tree that night, but saw nothing, and at first light, crept silently and unseen, to the pathway along the tall grass, where Slatolo was finally found, curled up tightly in death, the grass near him stained red by the blood that had flowed and pooled. Small spears with feathers tied at their bases protruded from him and from the ground near him. More were seen in the grasses nearby. The chief gathered these to bring back to the cave, and Mokolo and two other men lifted Slatolo and over the next two days, made their sorrowful way up the Valley and across the river to their home.

Later, in the sacred spot, a deep cleft high above the cave mouth, where many of the clan's dead had been carried and returned to the Great Mother, Mokolo stood silently crying as his father was laid among pine boughs and sent to rest beneath the earth. His spear and his knife were laid with him, as was his food gourd and water gourd.

The whole clan, including the Lesser Mothers, all the children and the Clan Mother gathered and sang the song of death over his resting place. As the last handful of earth had been put over him, the Chief Hunter approached, and thrust one of the small spears into the ground above him, saying "We shall all remember this day, and ask the Great Mother to remove our fear, soothe our pain and ask these new enemies to leave our valley home."

Mokolo remembered standing still near his father's resting place as the other men departed, until the sun had gone down behind him and the pathway back down to the cave became dark.

Mokolo thanked his father for every memory he carried. He quietly asked his father's spirit to guide him as he had when he was alive. He told him he was sorry for each time he disobeyed him, or lost his focus and let his mind wander. Finally, through his tears, Mokolo realized he'd said everything he had to say. He climbed up and over the ridge. As he was scrambling down the last few yards, the earth beneath his feet slipped away and he tumbled down from above, to land in a crumpled heap before the cave mouth. His shoulder throbbed in pain, but the pain in his heart was much worse. He hated those who had killed his father, and hated their small spears. He thought they must have been very small, to use such small spears, and the humiliation of his father falling to tiny men made him even angrier. He wished he could kill them. Kill them all.

The next days, not even the soothing of his own Lesser Mother could heal his heart. His friend, the maker Baaktolo found time to spend with him, helping him to rest, and listening to stories Mokolo would tell of his father, until the third day had passed, when it was no longer safe to speak of the dead. Any further speech about Slatolo would bring trouble to future hunts, and that night, Slatolo's death song was sung for the last time. Mokolo would always keep his father's memory with him, in his heart, but would not give voice to his name again. Slatolo's spirit had made the journey home to the Great Mother and his name had traveled with him. Forever gone, but now part of all life.

# # # #

The Chief of the Hunt had spent some days in seclusion, praying and cleansing himself, for he felt he had surely done something to bring this trouble to them. Datolo asked for forgiveness from the Clan Mother herself, after she granted him an audience to speak his mind. He had approached her sacred bed in the prescribed way, walking slowly backwards. He had taken further pains to cover his face with the dark grey mud of shame, as he was accepting the blame of the clan for the loss of a hunter.

She bade him sit in her ancient, low voice, asked him what had troubled his mind. He spoke carefully, without looking into her face and avoided mentioning the name of the dead, but those events that led up to the tragedy were

19

recounted, and he then laid the small spears he had gathered before her, on the white deerskin she sat upon.

The Clan Mother began to sing a deep, low song as she held up the small spears. Then she began asking them why they had been sent to kill one of the clan. She asked several times, always showing respect for the men who had made them, but finally, having not learned anything of their origins, quietly told the Chief Hunter that these were unknown things.

"These small spears have come from unknown men, and for that reason, you should wash the mud from your face. You did nothing to lead our hunter to his death. His death came from unknown enemies. Rise, Chief of the Hunt" She told him, "Your clan needs you. Wash your face and lead our men again."

He rose, thanking her, then again, backed away until he could turn and leave her sacred presence. She watched him go, her eyes moist with the tears she cried for them all. A loss of any member of her family was hard, and they were all her family. The loss of a hunter was especially troubling for them all, especially now that winter would be coming soon and meat would not be found easily.

Her eyes fell upon the three small feathered shafts lying before her knees, and she reached out and took one in her hand. She held it up so that the light of her stone oil lamp could play across its surface, highlighting the color of the feathers and the way the deer sinews were wrapped around its shaft to hold them. It was an ingenious device, she thought, having seen all manners of weapons made by men before. She especially marveled at the tiny stone knife that was placed carefully in the split end of the shaft, tightly tied with more sinew.

Despite its small size, the knife was very sharp, and she knew that it would go deep into an enemy, or into a four-leg. She had never seen anything like it before, and

wondered who the new enemies were and how they came
by these small spears. She especially wondered how they
could have thrown them so far and with such power that
they could remain unseen. Maybe it had to do with the
feathers tied to the base of the shaft – they seemed to be
the feathers of the large wandering water birds that came
to the river, spring and fall. They flew far and they flew in
large clans. Maybe their new enemies had tricked the
water birds to carry the small spears for them, or to give
their strong flight to the small spears through their
feathers? The Clan Mother puzzled over them until she
grew weary. She reclined, falling quickly into a fitful
sleep interrupted by dreams of loss and pain.

Chapter 4

The next morning, the problem of the small spears
still frightened her. As she held them in each hand, and
sighted along their shafts, she wondered how long it
would be before her entire clan would be threatened by
these small spears, or killed by them? She called to her
helper, the young girl Anas'kala, her own grand-daughter,
who appeared quickly from behind her shield boulder.
"Anas'kala? I will need fresh pine boughs and dream
grass. I must enter my dreams to find the Great Mother
and ask for her help. You must not speak of this, but…
our new enemies are greater than we, and have more
power. We will need to find a way to make peace with
them to save our clan and our home. Soon."

Anas'kala drew in her breath, fearfully, and answered
"Yes, of course Mother!" then hurried away, backwards,
to secure help in fetching the pine boughs and other herbs
needed to carry the Clan Mother into her dreams. Some of
these things were secret, stored far into the cave in places
no one but the Clan Mother and only a number, less than a
hand, of others knew – all women. She would need her
heavy skin cape, as the journey would lead her deep
through narrow, rock passages. She shuddered,
remembering the last time she'd been there, at the
beginning of spring. It was darker than night, and there
were smells and sounds she didn't recognize. The last
time, something silent had brushed against her in the
darkness, and she had to stifle a scream. There could be
no spoken words but those of the Clan Mother, and no
light at all may enter. She had learned that it was a place
very like the womb of the Great Mother who gave them
all life.

She moved quickly, with two helpers, along the
deepest passageway in the cave, until her hand, brushing
along the nearest wall, came into contact with a special,

pointed rock that protruded from the wall. She knew it
would be three steps more, then she would kneel at the
wall, and in the blackness, find the small opening that
would lead her to the sacred place. All the while, she
silently sang the song of new life she had been taught
since she was a young girl. Her helpers waited in the dark
while she squeezed herself into the narrow rock cleft, and
began wriggling her body through the opening into the
bones of the earth.

Ahead, she began to smell the pine boughs always
laid there, and disagreeable smells of other things, too. As
she wriggled into the sacred chamber, she lay down fully
prone upon the smooth rock floor, with just her feet
touching the edges of the opening behind her. Then, with
the silent song filling her mind, she was to reach both
hands directly out in front of her along the floor, until they
made contact with the special place that held the Mother
Seed. Once fully inside the rounded space, she could rise
up, on her hands and knees, and move to the front of the
special altar, where baskets of select herbs, mushrooms,
bones and the Seed awaited. Each would be carefully
retrieved and brought back out through the narrow
passageway, to the hands of her waiting helpers. Each
item would be brought out with its own silent song.

After all the other items had been passed out to her
helpers waiting at the cleft, the Mother Seed itself, would
be wrapped in white deerskin, in the darkness. This item,
she alone would handle, she alone would give directly into
the waiting hands of the Clan Mother. It took seven trips
into the narrow, suffocating chamber to retrieve these
things, but it was work she had trained for from her early
childhood and she was proud to do it perfectly, to bring
blessings upon the clan with her every movement and
thought.

As she and her helpers made their way back towards
the Clan Mother's waiting bed, they had thoughts of the

gravity of calling for these items at this time – not at a prescribed time connected to the moon, but now, as danger approached. Each sang the song of new life silently, perfectly, to insure the power of the prayers and dreams that would come to the Clan Mother and then, with her every breath, be passed on to every member of the clan. None of them had ever heard of the Clan Mother calling for these sacred items besides the moon times or the sacred sun ceremonies.

None of them had ever known any other Clan Mother, nor would they, but there had, in times long past, been other occasions when the sacred items had been retrieved in an emergency. The last was a sad time when their enemies, the bears, had taken three clan children in one day, and two more the following night. These were only ancient stories to the clan now, but it had happened.

The Clan Mother heard the three girls approach through the cave and for a moment, she let her memory return to the day when she saw her grand-daughter's face for the first time. She had known the joy and the pain of giving life many times, but only on those two special sacred times, when she gave life to another woman, could she recall each of their faces. Among the clan, she knew she was lucky to have been blessed to see her own daughter give life to another woman. Few lives ran long enough to see the children of children. Most passed on before their children grew to adulthood. She remembered the hunter who had just passed, and thought that if he had lived only a few more months, he may have known his own son would be sharing his seed for a new life. It was a blessing that so few had known.

The girls approached in the semi-darkness. Only the smoky fluttering light that came from her tallow lamp was allowed in her bed chamber. The girls, now all women who had seen their first moon time, but never lain with a man, arrayed themselves and their burdens in front of the

Mother's bed, upon the white deerskin which covered the floor. Anas'kala came last, and knelt down, her eyes upon the floor, holding out the bundle containing the sacred Mother Seed. It was heavy, and her arms began to shake with the effort, but as the Clan Mother began singing the song of new life in her low voice, the burden was lifted from her grand-daughter's shaking arms, honoring the pain of giving life.

The three girls rose, then backed away from the Clan Mother. When all three had turned behind the shield boulder and the room was empty save for her, the Clan Mother rose, with some difficulty. She was the oldest living member of the clan, and had become very fat, as she got little exercise. Her skin, she remembered from the last time she'd seen daylight – when she sang the death song for the departed hunter – was now an even, ghostly white, as was her hair, now trailing upon the floor as she rose. Her knees shook, so she waited a moment until the tremor passed before retrieving her lamp and a full water gourd from the near wall.

Her low voice, singing the song of new life, filled her bedchamber. She arranged the new pine boughs near her bed, then she returned to kneel upon her bed in front of the burdens the young women had placed upon the deerskin. Six baskets. Six different contents. One large wrapped bundle.

Arraying the pine boughs over her lap as she sang, she reached for the first basket. It contained dried leaves of Mountain Sage. She withdrew a sage leaf, then held it to her smoking lamp until the leaf caught fire, then shook it out, allowing its smoke to mingle with the smoke above her head. The stink of it made her eyes water, but she reached into the second basket. Dried flowers from the past spring and dried mushrooms. She withdrew a pinch of the flowers which she sprinkled into a small pile directly in front of her on the deerskin. She placed a single

25

dried mushroom nearby upon the floor and reached for the third basket.

The third basket was heavy, and contained dried blood from all her fertile moon times, now many years past. She took a pinch and sprinkled this too, in front of her in the same small pile. The fourth basket contained many locks of hair snipped from the heads of new baby boys before they had been washed and cleansed. It contained many generations. She withdrew a small lock of hair, and held it to her lamp until it too, caught fire and smoldered. This she lay upon the rock floor nearby, and then went into the fifth basket.

This basket contained the dewclaw hooves of fast-running fourlegs – their main source of meat. Each was taken from the first four-leg taken each spring, and it was considered an honor, by the hunters, if yours had been the first spear thrown. She removed one, curled and dried, and laid it next to the small lock of hair. Then, she shuddered slightly, as she reached for the sixth basket.

The sixth basket contained finger bones from all the Clan Mother men that had ever been. The basket was large and quite heavy. The bones had all been taken from the last Clan Mother at her death, by her heir – usually her own daughter or grand-daughter. She remembered trembling as she pressed the stone knife into her dead mother's finger, severing the last joint and nail. It was very hard, but the survival of the clan depended upon it, so she did what she had been raised to do.

This she kept in her lap. She lifted the heavy wrapped bundle next, and placed it also in her lap. Her song changed, becoming a low, secret song that she alone knew. It was in a language used only for this purpose, and told of the gift of life, and how all life within the clan was its expression. She began unwrapping the heavy bundle containing the Sacred Mother Seed. The deerskin was turned so that its hair was on the inside, facing the item it protected.

Finally, she withdrew a heavy, carved stone likeness of a pregnant woman, with wide hips and full breasts. The carving's arms were folded upon the chest above the breasts, and its heavy thighs met where a detailed carving of the origin of human life joined the full belly above it. This was placed reverently into the center of the small pile of flowers on the deerskin. The Clan Mother then picked up the dried mushroom and began to chew it as she removed her own skin and fur clothing, finally sitting opposite the figure quite resembling a larger version of the stone figure.

As she chewed, her song grew louder, her voice filled the room. Soon, as the mushroom's powerful alkaloids began to work upon her brain and nervous system, the song faltered, and she fell back onto her bed. Her breath coming in short gasps, she spoke her questions aloud through chattering teeth until all sensation left her. She slept on, gasping, fitfully, then after a time, lay very still almost as if she had died and left the clan unprotected.

Outside, her helpers waited, singing the song of new life silently as fatigue approached. They were trained to sing silently, and sit perfectly still, until the Clan Mother called again for them. It could take an entire day, sometimes more than a day, but in order to protect the clan while the Mother was walking in her dream state, far away from her People, the young women would follow their training.

Chapter 5

Mokolo was again scraping new spears in the fresh, morning air, two days later. He heard the hunters' song approaching up the trail, and turned to see Datolo's face beaming. Surely the chief Hunter's time with the Mother had brought them all blessings.

The blessings themselves followed as three fourlegs hung from saplings carried between hunters huffing and puffing their way up the steep trail, followed by the rest of the hunting party, now breaking into song. Hearing the hunters, several children and their mother men ran smiling out of the mouth of the cave to watch the spectacle unfold. Three fourlegs! That was amazing! The hunters gathered to lift the meat off the shoulders of those honored in the hunt.

The chief Food Mother strode forward with her large, sharp knife, and going to each deer in order, cut the throat and let some blood spill onto the ground while singing a song of thanks. With that, all the rest of the clan moved forward to help. The Food Mother's helpers carried large baskets, other men brought out knives and bone hooks. Mokolo and Baaktolo took up positions to assist as best they could, in carrying the freshly butchered meat back into the cool of the cave.

Other makers went about gathering green branches, bark and other firewood, under the old Fire Master's watchful eye. He directed several young men to a fire pit that had been set outside the cave, but near enough to keep watch on it through the night. Here he built a new fire, using pine logs and several green branches. Over this fire, not yet set ablaze, he erected, with the help of the two sentries, a large green willow grate on four legs. When it was set securely, he quickly brought a coal from the cave fire, and fanned it with tinder to set the new fire ablaze as well. This fire did not burn as brightly as the cave fire, but smoked a great deal. As it grew, more green boughs and bark were placed upon it, so the smoke it made grew heavy, tearing the eyes of those working to tend it.

Once the smoke started to billow, the Chief Food Mother brought out freshly cut strips of the deer meat to be laid upon the willow rack. In this way, two-thirds of the meat being butchered was dried on the smoke rack, preserving food for the hard months ahead. After the sun had fallen a bit from overhead, all the meat had been cleaved and divided, and the skins scraped clean, to prepare them for burial so that they could later be used for clothing. The legs of the deer were being stripped for their bones, hooves and their tendons. Not a single part of any animal would be wasted. Each clan member would be given as each had need.

For the next several days, there was a great deal of activity near the cave mouth, right through the nights, as both fires were tended, meat and skins smoked and prepared. Songs of thanks and celebration filled the air. There was dancing by the hunters, re-enacting each kill, and dancing by the women and children in thanks and when the clan slept, they slept with full bellies. Mokolo fell asleep on the bear skin bed with a satisfied smile on his face. Datolo the Hunt Chief slept easily this night, knowing he had been exonerated, and that the Great Mother had favored him, indeed, the whole clan, with the best hunt he could remember. His gnawing fear that he had displeased the Great Mother in the last hunt had evaporated and he drifted into a peaceful sleep for the first time since the last full moon.

Deep inside the cave, the Clan Mother bade her helpers depart for their beds. She was tiring sooner now. Even the happy times, the times of meat and feasting, tired her, and she knew that it would not be many full moons before she would have to leave the clan, called by the Great Mother to add her body to the earth, and sleep. As

she settled into her bear skin bed, she recalled the
blessings of the past few days and said a silent prayer of
thanks to the Great Mother, asking her for a little more
time to be sure her replacement was ready to take up the
work. She was suddenly distracted by a baby's cry,
coming from the closest group of mother men sleeping
just outside her sacred space, and fell asleep thinking it
was time to speak to Mokolo. Soon *his* seed would be
needed to replace that of his lost father.

Chapter 6

Four terrified deer burst from the tall grass first, followed by the runners. There were three does and a big buck with heavy antlers. All were tiring and showing the whites of their eyes in terror. They broke across the soft meadow grass and ran in a group towards the shelter of the trees with many deerskin-clad men right behind them. A series of tall poles had been driven into the ground on the hidden side of each bush or large rock, forcing the deer to follow a pre-determined pathway. Ahead, after a series of turns, five men waited holding long bows at the ready, their arrows nocked and strings half drawn. They were arrayed behind a line of low brush, just under the tree line, where shadows hid them.

As the buck and first two does broke from the carefully placed weir poles, they seemed momentarily confused, but a rush of flying arrows laid them down quickly. The fourth animal was also brought down by a flight of arrows soon afterwards. Two of the deer began struggling to regain their feet, but the men approached and quickly, with a short muttered prayer, cut their throats in simple passes with their finely flaked stone knives. The deer lay still and the hunters clapped each other on the back, and spoke of the successful outcome of their plan. The runners joined them and they began lashing the deer's legs to one of the sapling poles lying nearby at the ready.

"Anson was right!" the tallest hunter said with a bit of pride. "He knew it would work here just as well!"

His comrades smiled and nodded, one adding "The tall grass might have been a problem – it was hard to see them through it clearly, but our noise was enough to send them to flee!"

Each hunter carried his large stone knife in a flat pouch on a neck cord, so that it was always ready to use, always close by. They worked quickly and soon had all of

the deer, lashed by their crossed ankles to the poles. One
of the hunters stood on a bit of high ground, apart from
the work below, watching across the sea of grass and
beyond to the tree line and the rugged crags beyond. He
raised a hand flat over his brow to shield his eyes from the
sun and slowly turned back and forth across his field of
view.

"Anson!" called one of the hunters finishing with the
last deer. Anson slid down off the rocky knoll, his bow
carried across his back, and joined the other men. All of
the bows save his had been gathered together, as had the
remainder of the arrows. He and the younger hunter,
named Kells would be bringing the weapons home. He
would take the lead, as hunt leader, and Kells would bring
up the rear. Other men would be shouldering the heavy
burdens of fresh meat. They made ready to leave, back
along the trail they had followed into the Valley, from
beyond the lake.

Anson was still feeling very concerned about their
safety, and spoke to them "We must be wary in our return.
We knew there were bears, but saw none. We did not
know there were trolls, though." He shuddered,
remembering the first time he saw one of the hideous
creatures during the hunt last full moon. He continued,
"Trolls are worse than bears, and we must now always
pass silently and quickly out of this valley so that we will
not bring them along with us… back to our homes." To
make a strong impression on the younger hunters that did
not accompany them last time, he asked, "Who was it,
thinks he slew one of the trolls?"

An older hunter answered "I shot many arrows at the
one I saw through the grass, it screamed out, and there
was a great deal of noise, so I retreated, but in the
morning, when I got to where it had been standing, there
was only some blood. It wasn't dead, after all, just as you
said before."

Anson nodded, gravely. "We have all heard the old stories, about the trolls up in the high valleys. They are as tough as stone and our arrows and knives will not kill them. If we ever see them again, we must be silent, and not let them know we are about." He shook his head, adding "I'm very worried that they know us now and may soon follow behind us. Be watchful, all of you." with that, he turned and picked up the bundle of bows, slinging it over his shoulder. His own bow he carried in his free hand, at the ready. He strode up the way they had passed before, and the rest followed him with their heavy burdens. He was not pleased. It was a sorry turn of luck to awaken a troll's wrath and bring ruin upon your village.

The whispered stories of missing children and mutilated animals had terrified him as a boy, but since the last hunt, the enemy was real, not just a story. He'd seen them with his own eyes, and they filled him with dread. As the hunting party walked on, they moved silently, and every eye was watching for any sign they were being followed. The young hunter at the end of the line trailed a pine bough which he had tied to his waist with a long, braided cord. It cleared the path of footprints and any drops of blood from the game. It wouldn't do to announce their meat to every bear, wolf or hungry lion that might be prowling. Now, trolls, too. Anson's worries were many.

Chapter 7

Anson and his hunters had formed a small encampment for the night near the Valley's mouth, in an outcropping of huge standing rocks. Deep within the cluster was a small open space that would protect them from being seen by enemies, and also, one tall tree. The tree, Anson knew from past hunting forays, would be needed to haul up the meat to protect it from bears and other enemies. He saw that it had a strong fork, some distance from the ground, where a man might lodge himself to watch through the night. This was the task he gave himself.

As three of the hunters combed the nearby woods to search for firewood and anything that might help fill their bellies, Anson chose two other men to stand the first watch near the two entrances in the rocks which might allow access inside. "You'll both need to remain awake as long as you can", he told them, "but if you find sleep approaching, trade places with another to insure our safety."

The men nodded their understanding, and spoke quietly between themselves about the coming night and the threats it would bring. "Did you see them?" the younger man asked the other.

The older hunter nodded slowly, not wanting to mention it aloud. "I saw." he replied quietly, then added, "There were many, evil, cruel looking dark brutes. Much larger than a man, with burnt, black spears." he closed his eyes hoping that would satisfy his younger watch partner.

The younger hunter seem to suddenly pale as he heard. He asked "Can they run faster than we?"

"I don't know. It has been said that just seeing a troll will bring bad luck. Now I've seen many. Don't speak of it again." He laid his hand on the younger man's shoulder, then left to take up his position, across the clearing. The younger man, his eyes wide with fear, found a place to kneel down, and settled down at his post, his back against the rock behind him, his knife in one hand, his bow in the other.

Two of the hunters, the last to lay down their burden of meat, took long braided ropes from their belts, and began tying the deer's legs to the end of the rope, once they'd been removed from the carrying saplings. One of them climbed up the tree, as far as the fork, and caught the end of the paired ropes as his partner threw them up to him tied around a rock. He passed the rope around the nearest branch, then pushed it out along the branch as far as he could reach, before lowering the free end back down to the man below.

He climbed back down, and together, they raised the deer carcasses high into the tree. The ends were tied to a lower branch securely, and the next two deer were also raised high off the ground in the same manner. They must be raised three times a man's stature, as bears could easily be twice a man's height.

When it was complete, the men were both very tired, and looked for a place close to the fire, to sleep as best they could. They knew it would not be easy this night, with enemies all around them.

Anson told the hunter, Kells to prepare a small fire. "It must burn cleanly, with little smoke", he said sternly to Kells, who nodded.

Kells replied, "It matters but little, whether or not – they can smell us and our meat from the other side of the Valley if they are still there. They are probably much closer, just waiting for us to relax our watch"

Anson just replied, tiredly, "Either way, build it not to smoke, and keep plenty of wood and tinder nearby, in case we need it to flare high...later in the night."

Kells told him he'd be very watchful. He understood what Anson meant. Bears and trolls, too, even lions were afraid of fire, and a burning stick could be more useful than a knife in a fight against trolls. He began laying his pattern of twigs and tinder carefully in the long-prescribed manner. Other men returned with the firewood they had found, and the longer, drier logs were put into the fire from each direction, so they could be pushed in deeper as they burned.

The men kept their thoughts to themselves. Those whose women and children waited for them in their little homes were filled especially with the fear that the trolls or bears would follow them back out of the high valley and around the lake ... even to the village.

The sun dropped down behind the far ridge, to the West, sending deep shadows down into the small gorge in the rocks. A flickering fire provided a bit of light, as night began. The woods around them were silent, and full of potential enemies. Men glanced from their friend's faces to the fire, then fearfully outside the fire's protection, into the woods beyond, where darkness was growing. The oldest hunter, having survived many nights like this one, began unrolling his deerskin kit. It contained a remaining bit of dried meat, ground acorn meal and nuts along with a few dried berries from near the lake shore. He began to eat this from the palm of his hand.

Seeing him relax a little, the younger hunters also began unrolling their own and soon were quietly eating and muttering among themselves about the successful hunt, and the celebration that would greet their return. Anson, judging that all was in place for the night's safety, climbed up the tree to the fork, and secured himself in the most comfortable way he could. He withdrew the braided rope from his own belt, and tied himself securely within a web he wrapped about the branches and his legs. He left his arms free to use his bow – if need be. He hoped it would not come to that, and began watching and listening

to the woods around him for any sign that enemies were
nearby.

The fire sent flickering light up onto the rock faces
about the resting hunters. It interlaced with shadows of
nearby trees and danced across them in changing patterns
which unnerved the youngest hunters. Anson was satisfied
that little light was visible shining out beyond the rocks,
so he settled into his perch. There was little smoke and
very little talk from the men below. After several watchful
hours, Anson's weary eyes grew heavy and he fell into a
much needed sleep, despite the uncomfortable bed he'd
chosen for himself.

Chapter 8

The fire began flickering. It needed more fuel, so the older of the two sentries stood and wiped his weary eyes before walking to the edge of the firelit circle to retrieve another log. He nudged the man nearest to him awake. Whispering, "Come, help me with this log." The roused hunter wiped his eyes and stood, helping to drag the log to the edge of the dwindling fire. They raised the end nearest the fire and heaved it into the embers, end-first. It began to smoke and then caught suddenly in a bright flare.

The younger hunter told the older man, "Find your sleep. I'll wake and watch." The older man nodded, and returned to his small pile of boughs near the fire to warm up and find sleep. His companion resettled in his place, watching and listening for any night sound out of the ordinary. There was nothing he could hear beyond small mice and birds moving about beyond the circle of light, so he stretched his legs out and warmed the weary soles of his feet. Glancing around the circle of sleeping hunters, he caught the eye of the other wakeful hunter, on the far side of the fire. It now burned much brighter. The flames reflected on the other man's sweaty face, making the skin seem to dance. He turned his eyes back towards the narrow cleft between two of the rocks that had served as an entrance into this tiny stronghold. Nothing moved in the shadows beyond.

As he watched, he heard Anson, high above, moving in the tree. He was glad that unlike the Hunt Master, he was able to stay down here where he could relax and rest his bones. Along with the respect due him, Anson's task was full of hardship including the responsibility to guard the meat through the night. The wakeful hunter near the fire saw one sleeping hunter near him begin to rouse, shifting in his sleep.

The man pulled his feet in and sat up, wiping the sleep away. It was too early for him to take his turn awake, so he passed the wakeful hunter with a nod as he moved into the cleft between the rocks to release his water. The narrowing moon had risen and its light coated each tall rock with a silvery glow. The still sleepy hunter walked a bit further away from the circle of fire-light, and gazed out over the valley floor where just a tiny glint revealed the river below. A bird called out once, twice, then was still as the hunter relieved himself against the nearest huge rock slab.

Back within the firelight, the wakeful hunter thought he heard something slide above him and it brought him to instant, sharp awareness, but his eyes found Anson carefully wedged against the trunk above, so he relaxed. There! The soft, sliding sound came again, this time, closer to the cleft, but above it. He strained his eyes and stood, but could not see any movement above the protected circle of fire-light. As he was returning to his spot, the night was torn apart by the shriek of a man, then another. It brought them all to their feet in seconds. Each man's hand was upon his knife and some also clutched stout wooden branches, now clubs, still smoldering from the fire. The wakeful hunter and his partner from across the fire moved towards the cleft where the other hunter had disappeared only moments before.

"It was Raaka," he told the other, "He left to make water." They moved cautiously out from the fire-circle into the cleft. Just beyond it, in the moonlight, to one side of the path, they saw a large, dark stain upon the rock surface. One touched to sniff it and determine if it was blood.

"There's his piss. Where is he?"

They were answered by a sudden, painful scream from high above them, at some distance, ending in a moan that stopped suddenly. Anson, joined them near the cleft.

He had not seen anything, but had heard the sliding sound, too. He told other men it had reminded him of something he'd heard before. Soft, gentle. He'd think about it once they were all back in the fire-light. He laid his hands upon both of the other men's shoulders and pulled them back inside the cleft. Once inside, he gave the order to pile on the rest of the fire wood. He hoped it would last until the sun's return, but all were awake and sorely afraid. Their fear, he knew, would protect them until the light of day would help them find out what had happened to Raaka. He climbed back up to his spot in the trees branches while below, the remaining hunters, drew close together, their backs to the fire, their hands clutching their weapons.

Nothing more than a far-off rock fall was heard the rest of the night, and as soon as clear sight returned, Anson and Kells ventured through the cleft. The morning sun cast deep shadows about the opening where Raaka had disappeared. Nothing could be seen, beyond a disturbance in the pine needle floor of the forest, a step away from the rock cleft. Anson motioned silently to Kells, who moved up the slope above where Raaka had marked the stone face during the night. He cast his eyes over the ground from side to side, up the slope as far as he could, straining to catch something different in the texture of the forest floor.

Anson watched him move cautiously up the slope and he joined Kells as soon as the other man was more than two arms lengths away. It was their rule. Each protected the other from twice the distance a man's arm could reach. As he slowly moved upwards, he heard Kells slap his hand on his chest.

Kells stood pointing at something on the ground. When Anson joined him, he saw another disturbed area of the forest floor and a large dark pool, seeping into the ground. He reached out and it confirmed what he already knew. It was Raaka's blood. Disturbed gouges in the

40

forest floor left a trail: parallel marks of Raaka's heels being dragged over the ground. It led up to the top of the nearest huge rock, which sank into the slope behind, where it disappeared from view. The trail was marked with splashes and drops of blood. Bloody smears spread over the rock near its top. Anson moved away from the trail, to the side and moved up slope until he could see that it was safe atop the stone. Kells saw Anson point upwards, so he climbed up along the trail to the top of the stone. He stood and motioned Anson to join him, pointing at the ground below his feet.

When Anson joined him, he looked down at the answer to the soft sound he'd heard from his perch in the tree. Knife-Lion. Its huge paw prints were easy to follow in the soft sand atop the rock outcropping. They led directly up the slope and disappeared in the pine needles and undergrowth. Anson lay his outstretched palm over his heart. Kells did likewise and both said a silent prayer to the soul of Raaka, thanking it for its time with them and freeing it to continue its journey now that life was gone.

In a few moments, both men climbed sadly back down to the cleft, where one look at their faces told the tale to those gathered around the place where Raaka had left his water. Anson's thoughts swirled around and around in his head. Everything he thought of was accompanied by the soft noise in the night that had seemed to be beneath him. He wished he had recognized it then, and shouted an alarm. It might have saved Raaka, but he knew that what was… could not be changed.

Anson motioned all to follow him inside the shelter of the rocks. "We have a long day to travel before it is safe. Raaka was taken by a knife-lion. We honor his soul and the life he passed on, to all of us. His memory will be kept for many lifetimes and his song will be sung in every heart."

The other hunters each lay their own palms flat upon their chests, and silently spoke their thanks to Raaka's spirit. After a moment, they began putting their kit together for the long trek home. Anson and Kells lowered the meat and several hunters re-tied the lashings to hold it on poles. In a single-file line, they walked past the place where Raaka's life ended, and returned to the faint pathway through the forest, still protected from clear sight by the morning shadows.

Three deer made it a good hunt, but the loss of Raaka made it a very costly one. As they walked, Anson leading, ever watchful, each one held his memories of Raaka close. His name would only be spoken aloud, when the village gathered to pray and honor his memory. A song would be sung. The Raaka song that would shelter his memory and comfort his spirit. His woman and his father would need to be told first, and that was another of the hardships that the hunt leader had to bear.

Chapter 9

Nils' face was as dark as his thoughts. Anson watched his village chief pace back and forth across the hard-packed earth floor. Finally he stopped and stared up into the ceiling beams, asking Anson, "…and you saw no other lion tracks the whole hunt?"

"No, my chief, none. I had kept my eyes sharp for them and for bear as well, but we only saw the tracks of the deer we followed." Anson had worried that Raaka's loss might be his fault. He'd wracked his brain trying to find one moment of weakness... one moment he had relaxed his watch and missed a paw print or tuft of hair in a thorn bush, or bird warning, or… it did no good. He kept returning to the soft sound he'd heard from the tree.

Nils crossed his arms over his chest, then asked, "Nothing at all, besides that sound you told me you heard?"

"No" came the reply. Nils nodded, then turned again and strode a few paces, his hand clutching his beard as he turned the event over and over in his mind. Finally, he approached Anson, clasped him on both shoulders and told him, "It wasn't your fault. The sound alone of something soft sliding over rock would not have alerted anyone. It was Raaka's time. Knife-Lions happen."

Anson was much relieved. He ventured a smile as Nils added, "…and you led a very good hunt. Three deer is a count your father would have been proud of!" Nils clapped him on the shoulders again. Then, he reached up and stroked his own beard again, turning away. Anson recognized this as something the chief did when he was about to ask a question, so he waited.

"No trolls this time? Not even footprints?"

Anson knew where this was heading. The old tales said that trolls traveled only at night, which was one of the reasons the hunt had been so surprised by coming across them the last moon. It was late in the day, but the sun still held the sky above them all when it had happened. Nils wanted to make sure the hunting party had not been passed in the dark, then followed, bringing trolls out of the high valley and down to the lake. He answered with as much confidence as he could muster. "No my chief, there were no footprints, we saw no trolls or trollsign."

"Good. Very good, Anson. Thank you for leading this excellent hunt. The game in the high valley is much better than what we have nearby, so if your hunters keep bringing in three or even more deer, we'll all have full bellies this coming winter."

Nils turned back towards his house fire, and Anson clapped his chest with his outstretched palm and turning to the door, lifted the bearskin and stepped over the threshold into bright sunshine. He saw women gathering up their children and pushing them towards the village fire-circle, in the very center of the small community. The primary family houses radiated out from it in each direction and the spaces between each were planted in small vegetables, mostly roots for the winter, and medicine plants. The fire-circle was a large pit lined with flat stones and ringed by larger stones with a raised platform of stone leading away towards the lake. The platform now was spread with bearskins and lion skins, and soon, Anson knew, the ancient Seer would take his place there, to sing Raaka's song. The entire village would gather around Raaka's woman and his father's family and honor them with their songs and prayers.

Anson had only a short time to get to his house, two rows back, and return with his woman and their three children. Glancing back as the Seer's helpers brought firewood into the pit, he hurried to get home. He would be expected to speak about Raaka's honor, his skill and his last fight with the lion, but Anson had no idea what he would say. The soft, sliding sound was all he heard in his mind, over and over again. And Raaka's screams, of course, but he wouldn't speak of that.

Gudrun was waiting for him at their door. "Hurry, Anson! You're still all muddy! What's that on your sleeve, blood?" she cried in a horrified tone. He might have been the leader of the hunt, but here, Gudrun was chief, and he smiled weakly. He embraced her quickly and they went inside. She was already dressed in her finest deerskin dress, with the quillwork across her bosom, her legs wrapped in whitest deerskin and her golden hair in thick, twin braids coiled up on the sides of her head and held with her finest bone combs. She was beautiful and made him so proud he stood taller when he was at her side, before the families' council. But here, her tongue was often sharp-barbed, so he tried to dress quickly. He told her the story of Raaka's death, while he pulled his muddy deerskin shirt off over his head. She brought him a small pottery basin of water and he knelt down and washed his face and arms, then pulled the fresh, quill-embroidered shirt she brought, over his head, smoothing out the sleeves on his arms. He hadn't seen this one before. It was new.

"Thank you. This shirt should be worn by a chief, it is so wonderfully made, and the decoration is truly amazing. You are too good to me."

"Don't I already know that?" she replied with a smile, adding, "...but you are leader of the hunt, and you should look as well as you can."

Their two girls came skidding through the skin door flap with their taller brother chasing behind them.

"Don't you get all dirty again!" Gudrun shouted, and they froze in their tracks. Haakon, their eleven year old son, asked, "Are you finally ready to go? We've already seen the fire." His sisters nodded their heads fiercely in agreement. "Can we go now?" they pleaded.

Gudrun put up her finger, waiting for Anson to nod, then he strode out first, followed by Gudrun , then Haakon with the girls following in size order. He adjusted his pace to reflect the somber occasion, but the children were so excited, they fidgeted and ran into their mother's skirt several times on the way down to the fire circle. As they walked, other families joined them until a crowd moved through and past the last primary family house and on to their respective places around the fire circle, near stones marked with the shape of the animals whose spirits led their family clans. There were only hushed voices, then total silence as the last families made their way to their places near the fire.

When the fire circle was ringed by all 63 members of the village, the chief and his two women, along with their five children, took their place at the back of the stone platform. The remaining area, nearest the fire on the platform was left for the Seer and his helpers. Once the chief was seated, they made their way slowly up to the fire circle from the shore of the lake, where they kept their own fire-circle and house. Everyone held their tongues as the Seer's helpers came first, bearing the remaining possessions of Raaka, wrapped in white deerskin, his broken bow and his knife atop the bundle. They lay it down next to the fire circle, then the Seer ascended the platform, and took his seat directly behind.

He motioned for the heads of the families of the village to stand, and in a loud, sad voice, asked each, "Why have you come here today with your family?"

Each answered, "To remember and honor of the deeds of Raaka and sing of his skill and his passing into the world of spirits." Then each man took his seat with his people and the question would be asked of the next in line until it had been answered ten times, once for each family clan.

The Seer then looked up to the clouds, both palms spread, thumbs touching and said. "We have heard the ten families. Raaka has left us, but we hold his memory close to our hearts." Lowering his eyes, he asked the gathered people, "Who among you was Raaka's friend?" At this, a few sniffles and muffled cries were heard, from his woman and from other men who had been closest to him. One by one, someone would stand, saying "I was Raaka's friend. I remember and honor his memory." Each would add a small story from Raka's life, and so it went until the Seer asked the chief to stand.

By this time, wailing was heard from many women and younger children, upset to see their mother men crying. Nils stood, then strode over to where Raaka's belongings lay and picked up his broken bow. He asked aloud, "Who among us will speak of Raaka's last battle? Who was there?"

Anson stood. As leader of the hunt, this was his responsibility. He clapped his outstretched palm to his chest in respect and began telling how Raaka had been the most skillful with his bow that day, and had pulled his arrows from all three of the deer. His discussion focused upon the hunt and past hunts, then only at the very last, mentioned how a knife-lion had set upon Raaka in the dark and dragged him away -- "...Yet we heard him fight the beast until he drew his last breath, such was his great strength. Raaka was a great hunter and a strong man whose honor will live forever!" Anson hoped he had spoken well. The last phrase was one always used, and it pleased him to see faces in the crowd nod their heads and clap their palms on their own chests.

Anson took his seat with Gudrun as the Seer began singing in a deep, melodious tone, the song of Raaka, hastily cobbled together down by the lake shore, only hours before. He sang it four times, once for each direction. On the fifth cycle, the Seer's voice was joined by the voices of as many of the gathered people as could remember the words, all joining in when the name, Raaka, was called at the beginning of each verse. The fire kindling was lit by the Seer's helpers and when the flames began to shoot up higher than a man stands, the helpers gathered up Raaka's bow, his knife and belongings, and heaved the bundle into the growing flames. It all burned until long after dark, when all the families had returned to their homes.

Chapter 10

A new moon rose as the Valley floor darkened. Full
and sleepy, Mokolo wanted to lie in his bed, but he
listened as he must, to the low, moaning clan song. It was
being sung by the Lesser Mothers and its tones had always
been the last thing he heard before sleep took him as he
grew up. Every night, they would sing the song their clan
had sung at day's end, while the light fled. He wished the
Lesser Mothers would hurry, none the less. He needed
sleep. It had been a very busy day for him. A proud day,
but a day of fear.

He'd been roused early, while it was still dark, by
Datolo, the Hunt Chief, who put his finger over Mokolo's
mouth. It meant, do not speak. They crept past the fire and
the fire tenders who sat staring into the flames and
dissolved into the shadows at the back of the cave, near
where the Lesser Mothers and girls slept. They were met
by the Clan Mother's helper, who told them to follow
quietly, to a place that had been prepared. He knew what
he must do. Each young boy had been told, many times, of
this morning and of the time they would spend with the
Clan Mother. Alone.

Mokolo stepped carefully, lest he kick a stone and
waken any sleepers. The girl led them into a small side-
passage and bade them sit upon a bed of pine boughs
which had been prepared. A small fire glowed, giving its
light to the tiny space and coloring everything a dull red.
The sacred color of blood and life. The helper began to
back out of the passage, while singing quietly, a song of
life. They waited.

Soon, the girl returned with two deerskin wrappings,
which she placed around each man's eyes. Both knew
they could not look upon the Clan Mother without
bringing evil upon them all. They heard the girl leave,

then after a short time, they heard the deep, rumbling voice of the Clan Mother asking if a man had come to her.

Datolo spoke. Mokolo knew that it would have been his father who brought him, but... He shuddered and waited. The Clan Mother and Datolo exchanged the words that had always been said, then lying his hand on Mokolo's shoulder, he slipped out of the passageway and returned to wait for the new day. Mokolo was alone in the darkness, then he heard the sound of someone approaching. It nearly took his breath away, as he heard the Clan Mother join him upon the pine boughs. She touched his shoulders with both hands. Then his chest, then his thighs. He knew what was coming and hoped he would not fail. She began a low song that echoed around the stony passageway. As she sang, she lifted his breechclout, and he felt dry, warm hands cradling his man spear and his stones. She sang of the gift of life and the man seed that brought it. She was very gentle, but after her repeated stroking, his spear grew quickly. He felt the tension of fear but also the pleasure he had known when alone. After a time, he knew his seed would soon spurt out. He hoped it would be very strong. As his breaths came quicker, he gasped and his seed spilled into the waiting hand of the Clan Mother. She thanked him, and told him that now he would be called upon to renew the clan.

In the near-darkness, the Clan Mother held Mokolo's semen in her hand and reached down to grasp the Mother Seed, from where it had lain nearby. She rubbed the contents of her hand all over the surface of the Mother Seed, back and front. When she was finished, she told him, "Mokolo, you are a man, full and strong. All of the Mother men have been honored by your deeds and your love for your clan. Soon, you and your seed will be given to the Mother that will bear your children. It is a new day for the clan, and a new day for Mokolo. We all will rejoice." She again laid her hands upon his chest, then his shoulders, and then she departed, with the gift of his seed. He hoped it had been enough. He waited for her to leave.

After a few minutes, he heard the Clan Mother's helper call him forth, and he removed the wrapping around his eyes. The small fire still glowed red, and he stepped out of the passage, smiling. The girl motioned for him to follow. When he stepped out into the larger part of the cave, where all the clan could gather, he found them all waiting for him and smiling. He was now a man. Full and strong. The Lesser Mothers all were gathered against the wall. His own stepped forward with tears falling from her eyes and cried out that her son was now a man. The other Lesser Mothers circled around her and embraced her while the men all stepped forward and clapped him on the back. Smiling, talking. Mokolo felt proud and happy, but he wished his father had been the one to bring him to the Clan Mother.

Later that day, when the feasting and singing had concluded, he felt a light touch upon his arm, and Datolo was there telling him to follow him. They had something of great importance to discuss. Alone.

Mokolo wondered if he was going to be given to a young, Lesser Mother, but Datolo just shook his head and replied with a laugh, "Soon enough, your time will come. This is about something besides your man spear!"

Chapter 11

"Are you sure of that?" Ariel Conner had been trying to push her excitement down for days now. This was just too much. Completely unexpected. Since the full genomes had been completed, she'd hoped for just this kind of opportunity.

"Listen, come down to the lab and see for your self – it glows, really strong." Three lab assistants had gathered to bring her the news. The trip would take all of six minutes, to the next building, so she lay down her pen and told them she'd be along in a few minutes. They disappeared quickly, their own enthusiasm driving them.

Ariel straightened the papers on her desk as the thoughts of the big disappointments of the past few years intruded. The rejection of her initial doctoral thesis came unexpectedly. Professor Williams – Jesse – had almost guaranteed her that despite her new ideas about mingled genes, her paper would be a "*breath of fresh air*". Those were his words. He'd had little to say when the committee sent her back to square one. Less than little.

After three Summers of work, she'd begun finalizing her theoretical ideas about the origins of racism and all those monster stories told to children. Northern Europe folklore was particularly rife with such tales. It spoke often of shadowy predators like giants, trolls, ogres and the like; clearly devised to keep children and plain people closely reined in and near their rulers for protection. That much was the common theory, but Ariel had new ideas.

She'd gathered material from the oldest oral traditions all over Scandinavia and Northern Germany until she had what she believed were solid clues. She believed these clues led to a completely new theory of how Northern Europe, in fact, most of the larger land masses on the planet were populated by the human species.

"*Ms. Connor, you may have found elements of culture that you interpret this way, but you really have no actual evidence. Nothing that would convince the community that your conclusions are sound. In its present form, we cannot tell you to proceed with your paper, in all good conscience.*" Those were the words of the Dean of Sciences as the doctoral committee rejected her proposal. Those were the words that she would hear over and over again in her mind, every time she got close to anything that encouraged her.

She had taken another full year to re-tool her thesis, more in keeping with the canon of thinking that the University relied upon. She also lost the fellowship she'd been offered. Jesse, too. He quickly found a more entertaining student to… mentor. After completing the post-grad work on her doctorate, she found a TA job in Oslo which soon became a full faculty position. Still, thinking about the years she had wasted, occasionally kept her sleepless. *Keep it under control*, she told herself, then gathered up her briefcase and purse, and left her office.

The Spectroscopic Lab was shared by several disciplines in the Earth Sciences and with both anthropology and archaeology, so time was at a premium. The relics they had recovered in Norway had been undergoing analysis for several weeks, including carbon dating sampling. Since the discovery of so much useful material within the cleft cave – called by a less than scientific name by the male lab assistants – she was getting the distinct impression that some of her geology colleagues were getting a bit impatient.

"Just wait 'til you see this. You're not going to believe it!" Her lead technician Grant, was clearly stoked.

Inside the outer office, the side chairs were filled with anxious technicians. They all stood when she entered behind Grant, and crowded around the narrow doorway into Lab 4. There was only room for a very few of them inside and the door's window had been sealed with black foamcore and tape, so there was nothing for those remaining outside to watch. Still, after the door closed, they remained standing and whispering excitedly amongst themselves while the procedure was repeated for Dr. Conner.

The room was as dark as the cave had been. Totally black. She took a deep breath, reached out to find the edge of worktable, and said, "OK." The table was flooded with ultraviolet light from a focused source and upon it lay a large, finely worked stone female form. The carving glowed bright greenish-white across its entire surface, brighter in the crevices and deep recesses.

"My God! It's... it's unbelievable. How old did you tell me the deerskin wrapping was?"

Grant replied, "Let's see... I think this one was somewhere between 36K and 39K, B.C. E. Other layers were older. The oldest one was... let me check."

He switched on the overhead light and shut down the UV. He flipped through several cli-boarded pages that had been lying on the work surface. "The oldest was more than 10K older." He tapped the data notation on the summary in confirmation, smiling.

The object on the worktable lay there in all her deep brown glory. She – they now called them all "she"-- was 30 cm long and 20 cm wide. She was a carved, nude female figure, similar to others that had been recovered over the years, especially in Neanderthaler sites in Germany, but slightly different in her pose. This figure's hands were folded over her chest, above heavy breasts. Her arms remained tight to her torso and her breasts rested on a huge, protruding belly which fell away to well-rendered female parts and fleshy thighs and legs. Her face was blank with the exception of a knotted coil of what they guessed was hair and deeply sunken eyes under protruding brows. She had been painstakingly carved from a travertine-like rock, but was covered with many layers of an applied powdery substance.

Most of the similar work found previously was smaller and uncoated, found lying loose within a dig stratum or in a rocky niche. Some of them were recovered from niche burials. Some were clay, some were tufa or limestone. Most had been dated to the Middle Stone Period, but this one was much more recent and had been found, along with five other, smaller figures, preserved, tightly wrapped in grasses and deerskin, within root fiber baskets inside the narrow cleft in the Norwegian cave system her team had excavated just a few months past. There had also been many baskets containing seeds and what must have been herbs or food stuffs. Some of the baskets were sealed with pitch. One contained hundreds of human finger bones. Neanderthaler bones. It had been a major discovery, but this UV testing was producing a bumper crop.

Ariel pulled on a pair of Nitrile gloves from the nearest dispenser, and gently lifted the object, to place it under a large magnifier. She looked up at Grant and asked him, again, "…and you tell me it was just a chance mistake?"

"Of course, we weren't going to do a UV light test, but the light had been inadvertently left on over the work table when we brought it into the lab to remove the covering. Who would have expected this?"

Ariel gave it a few moments' thought, then asked, "Did it come right up when the deerskin was removed?"

"No", said Grant, "no one noticed until we flipped off the lights to leave, then there was a very faint glow from the recessed areas and crevices. We brushed the surface, and got more glow, until we were able to get the entire surface to fluoresce."

"Did..?"

"Yes, yes, of course, we keep every bit of the powdery substance. It will need testing, no?"

"DNA testing, yes." As they left the lab, she added, "You'll let me know the second the results come in, won't you?" Grant nodded, a huge grin spreading across his face.

She stifled a rapidly approaching... conclusion. There was no precedent, but still... Ariel needed to think and to walk. She thanked Grant and left the lab, walking quickly down the nearest corridor that led outside.

Grey clouds were scudding overhead and a breeze picked up the loose leaves, swirling them against the masonry wall. *This is going to point towards...* she stopped her mind again, always the intuitive thinker, it just wouldn't do to decide before the test results were in.

After a few more strides, as she reached the corner of the lab building, the thought struck her again. *If this testing shows Neanderthal DNA, it points exactly where my thesis would want it to: Here it is. Ten thousand years later than when the Neanderthal bloodline should have been gone from Northern Europe.* She couldn't suppress a smile that began to creep over her lips. If this were true, then it would also follow that the two species knew of each other, even lived near each other. *How does their contact still affect us now?* She couldn't banish the feeling that her ideas were about to be proven.

Chapter 12

Mokolo held the small spear up so the light of the sun would shine from behind it. The fletching at the notched end glowed. He looked closely at the way the feather had been sliced, then attached with pitch and wrapped at each end. There were three feather sections. He turned the shaft and sighted down along it towards the end where the tiny knife was lodged in the split and wrapped. The light played down perfectly evenly. The shaft was perfectly straight. It had been scraped from a larger shaft to make it so. He lay the small spear down upon the ground and wiped his eyes.

It had been four days since he'd spoken with the Clan Mother. He was still deeply shaken by the experience following the seed ceremony. He had followed Datolo into another side passage where food was stored. They were greeted by the Clan Mother's helper who bade them sit and wrap their eyes again. Soon, he was hearing again, from the Clan Mother herself. Mokolo.

He had been chosen, she said, because of his skill as a maker of spears, She was worried, and wanted him to try to make some small spears, like the one she passed on to him, wrapped in a piece of deerskin. "Do what you can to make them as close to the one I have given you. Datolo will then try to throw it from a great distance and see if it is possible to have it fly straight, further than a spear could be thrown. Speak to no one about this. It is a grave matter. The survival of our clan may depend on what you can do, so be very patient and careful as you work."

Those were her last words to him before she left them. Her helper had told them, once outside the passageway, that the Clan Mother would expect to hear from Datolo within one hand of days. Mokolo only had one left. He picked up the best of the small spears he had tried to make. It wasn't perfectly straight, but almost. The feathers were different, also. No large waterbirds were still at the river. They had taken their tribe away, as they did each year, and would not be back until the earth woke from winter again. Many full moons yet to rise. He had found only one of their wing feathers, but part of it was old and rotted. He had used the biggest feathers he could find, but they were not as long or as stiff as the ones on the spear the Clan Mother had given him.

When Datolo had tried to throw it using a spear thrower, it only flipped over in the air, or flew a short, erratic distance. Datolo said that the men who made the small spears must be either very small, or they must have something else to throw the small spears. Not a throwing stick. That seemed to Mokolo to be impossible. There was no other way to throw a spear a long way. If there was, Datolo would know. He was worried that the Clan Mother would not be pleased with what he had made. It would shame him. It might hurt the Clan.

He picked up the first small spear, again, and this time he looked down at the end that was notched. It seemed that something very narrow would fit in that notch, but what could it be? A thin throwing stick would not be accurate or strong enough. He puzzled over the problem as the sun began to fall towards the far ridge. He had one more day to find an answer. He hoped the Clan Mother was praying to the Great Mother to send him wisdom.

As the sun dropped behind the far ridgeline, Mokolo saw Datolo approach slowly, carrying several of the small spears he had made and his throwing stick. He was not smiling, so Mokolo decided to rise and join him for the return to the cave. They could speak on the way. Maybe an idea had come to Datolo, but it didn't look like it from the dark expression his face was wearing.

"Mokolo," he called out, as the two approached each other, "There must be spirits in the first small spear that carry it. There is nothing I could do to make it fly where I wanted it to, and still fly far."

Mokolo nodded, averting his gaze from the older man's eyes. "Maybe I'm not making them right," he offered.

Datolo stopped, and said, "Wait. Let me try something. Do you have the first small spear?"

Mokolo handed it to him. Datolo held it in one hand and lay down the bundle he'd been carrying, choosing from it the very straightest, best version of the small spears Mokolo had made. He stood up and turned to face a large tree near the trail. It stood the length of six men or so away from them. He took the first small spear and held it as if it were a large spear, overhead, but with his thumb and forefinger instead of his whole hand, then threw it to strike the tree. It flew straight and struck the tree with a pop. The small knife at its end had bitten deeply and the arrow remained in the tree's tough bark. Datolo nodded, then turned to Mokolo, saying ,"Now yours." He did the same with the best of Mokolo's small spears, and it too, flew straight and stuck in the tree, quivering.

"You see, your small spears are as good as the first small spear. They fly straight and bite deep."

Mokolo smiled. Their power wasn't in the way he made them at all. He replied, "Then, it must be in the way they are thrown. The other men know a way to do it. We must find their way to throw."

He and Datolo discussed it as they returned to the cave. Both had considered a thin throwing stick, but neither could determine how it would be held to make the small spear fly straight. Datolo was not convinced that a way could not be found, so he said he would make a very thin throwing stick that would fit in the first small spear's end notch. Mokolo agreed.

"We can try. Maybe new wisdom will come when we are making the new thin ones."

59

Datolo clapped him on the back, saying, "You made good small spears. Now we just need to find out how to throw them far. We'll find the answer, don't worry."

But the next day, they hadn't found the way, and when they went to speak with the Clan Mother again, they wore sad faces and carried bad news.

Chapter 13

"It is the only way left to us, but it will not be safe for you. I cannot go with you to protect you. I am too old, but I can send my helper, to carry my blessing and be my eyes." The Clan Mother added, "You will leave with the sun, in the morning. My prayers will go with you."

Mokolo and Datolo walked into the large part of the cave, their eyes blinking to adjust to the bright firelight. Mokolo started to speak, but Datolo stopped him, saying, "There is no other way for us. But we will be three. Three is better than two or alone."

They ate the evening meal in silence, sitting away from the other men, who spoke and pointed, wondering what was going on between them. And why they had gone to the women's part of the cave so many times. Mokolo's friend, the maker Baaktolo, watched them eat. A man near the fire made a joke about Mokolo's seed ceremony, and several men laughed until Baaktolo said, "Stop. That will bring shame on us all." The man who made the joke gave him a sour look, but returned to discussing the next hunt. Baaktolo watched his friend and the Hunt Chief speaking quietly, but knew that as they had left the group, the discussion was private. It did not concern him. He turned his eyes back to the fire. Whatever the two were discussing, would wait until he was told. Secrets didn't last long among them.

As the sky outside the cave's mouth began to brighten. Mokolo felt a hand upon his shoulder and woke easily. To tell the truth, sleep had not come all night. He was anxious for the day to begin. All night he had thought about the problem, but despite all the time he considered it all, nothing came to him. He rose and joined Datolo at the fire. Datolo had prepared a bundle of food, wrapped in deerskin, a bundle of the new small spears Mokolo had made, six large spears and several throwing sticks.

"Bring a skin for warmth.," he told Mokolo, "the night was cold. The next may be colder."

They finished their morning meal as the sun was just beginning to light the trees. "Come, we must leave." said Datolo.

"But where is the Mother's Helper?"

Both men glanced around the cave and found the young woman striding from the darkness to meet them wrapped in a bear skin and carrying a large bundle slung over one shoulder.

"Here she comes." The young woman nodded to acknowledge the men, but motioned for them to join her and the three stepped out on the wide dirt apron beyond the cave's mouth, where she made her morning prayer and spilled a pinch of pollen for the sun's blessing. In less than an hour, as the sun broke from behind the tree lines above them, they were miles away. They walked quickly and silently at the edge of the forest. Hand gestures were all the communication they needed, as the plan had been carefully explained by the Clan Mother.

"The Great Mother watches you and will bring you to the... other men. Follow down the Valley, the direction the river flows, but stay out of sight, near the forest. Make no noise. Continue down until you find other men, and watch them from afar. Your eyes will be blessed by the Eagle and your legs will be blessed by the fleet fourlegs' spirits. Remember all you see, and bring it back to me."

The first night, they stopped near a huge deadfall, where the hunters had stopped before, for shelter. Deep, under the overhang of the dead roots, was a cozy shelter. They were all footsore and tired, but they each wondered how they would spend the night, since one of them was a woman. Again, the Clan Mother had told them how it would be. Her helper would not sleep the first night. She would chew the grey leaf and it would keep sleep away. If danger came, she would wake them. Each night, a different one would not sleep, until they returned. She sent much grey leaf with them.

The closeness that might occur taking shelter together, she told them, would not bring shame upon the Clan because they had been told to do so by Their Clan Mother, and because there would be no coupling or close touching except by the necessity of the journey and they would not speak to each other except by necessity when they were sure no one would hear.

"You will be silent, unless you must speak. You will know when it is right to speak. I send my prayers with you. Learn and tell me when you return."

Mokolo fell asleep, wrapped in a wolf skin, commanding himself to learn. Learn everything. Return to tell the Clan Mother. Before he closed his eyes, he ventured a careful glance at the Mother's Helper. She sat near, with her back to the two men, who were curled close together, beneath the overhang. Mokolo had watched how her hair shone in the sun as they traveled and now, could smell her, she was so close. *She has a sweet, wonderful smell,* he told himself, finally closing his eyes.

Datolo's hand woke him the next day, and they continued their travel in the same way, until the sun began to sink. They had come further than any hunts Datolo could remember, and began seeking some kind of shelter for the coming night. Just before the sun was gone completely, they saw a group of large rocks leaning together with a small, dark opening beneath them. As they approached, they smelled the air to be sure no other men were about, or bears, or lions. They had seen no tracks of enemies or other men, but as they approached the rocks, they smelled burned wood. In the depression beneath the rocks, a fire pit had been dug, and it still held ashes from a fire.

Datolo rose, with a troubled look, and gazed out over the Valley, looking for any sign of other men, but none

63

was seen. He motioned with his hand flat and his palm down, and moved his arm across his chest, then put two fingers over his lips. It meant he saw no one, but they must remain silent. He pointed at the fire pit, making a zigzag motion of his outstretched hand, and both Mokolo and the woman nodded slowly. They knew it was not a fire pit their own hunters used, but it had been a long time since a fire had burned there, so they decided, clapping their hands slowly to their chests, that they would spend the night under the small shelter the rocks provided.

Mokolo was next to chew the grey leaf, and as the other two slept, he stared out at the darkness. When the moon rose, the valley floor was lit in silver and he saw the river was clear and bright. He heard the familiar night sounds of fourlegs rustling in the brush below them, the skittering of the small tree animals and an owl's calls. He heard the first songs of crickets, too and they comforted him through the night. He carefully listened for any other sound, especially one made by a larger animal, but all that night, he heard only the sounds of safety. They were protected from above and behind them anyway, and with no fire, they could not be seen by other men.

As dawn broke, though, all three were suddenly alarmed by the sound of a rock slide, far above them on the mountain side. They rose and turned to face the sound as it slowed and finally stopped. None of them moved. They listened for any other sound that might mean a large animal or men were moving above them, but nothing more came. Datolo motioned for them to sit to eat the morning meal, and when they were finished, he stood and walked a few yards out from beneath the sheltering deadfall to search the Valley for movement.

Mokolo watched him carefully surveying the Valley floor, and saw him suddenly stop to stare at one spot. Mokolo rose and joined Datolo. The older man pointed down to where a narrow stream branched off from the river. There was a large rock coming out from the bank, and there… right on top of the rock, was a bear. Mokolo felt the fear climbing up his back. Nearby, after a few moments, they saw another. The bears were fishing, so it would be safe for them to creep past far above them. The bears would not pay attention to men passing if there were fish to catch. Mokolo relaxed a bit and reaching into his bag, he found a piece of dried meat which he began to chew while he watched the bears fish.

The bear on the bank suddenly lunged into the stream and ducked his head beneath the water, coming up with a big, silvery fish struggling in his teeth. He backed up the bank and threw his catch on the ground, pinning it with his paw as he began to feed. The other bear was still on the rock, watching, when he suddenly stood on his two legs, looking behind him and sniffing the air. Mokolo knew the bear had heard or smelled something, both he and Datolo looked in the direction the bears nose pointed, to see what had spooked him. After a moment, they saw the high grasses parting in several places behind the bear and saw the bear begin swatting at the air as if there were flies bothering him. But these were no flies. In a few more moments, the bear toppled down off the rock into the stream. The other bear had begun running away from the grass, jumping across the stream and into the river, upstream. The last Mokolo saw of him, he was swimming across the river to the other side, far above where his friend lay still in the water of the stream, now running red with blood.

Then the other men came from the grasses, climbing down the bank to the bear with knives held in front of them. There were six of them. They approached the bear and one hit the bear with his fist. The bear did not move. Three more of the other men joined their fellow and the four pulled the bear from the stream by his legs. Once the bear was on the bank, other men began pulling out small spears. It had taken many of them to kill the bear, but the bear had not threatened the other men, that Mokolo could see, and he wondered why it had been killed. His clan would not kill a bear unless it had hurt or killed one of their clan, or if it was threatening them. These bears had only been fishing. It troubled him.

Datolo and the Mother's Helper were now pulling him back to cover, where they could watch unseen. They knelt behind a large growth of brush and watched other men open the bear up and begin removing its skin. There were other signs that troubled them all.

Other men were tall and very thin, not tiny. They wore what looked like deerskins all over themselves, including their legs. Their hair was very long, two pronged, and it was the color of honey! But it was their faces, were the most puzzling. Their faces were the color of a four-leg's bottom! They were all white, like a cloud! Mokolo felt the fear climbing again. Maybe they were spirits. Their faces had no color... no, one of them had a red face. The one pulling the skin from the bear's back. His hair was darker than the rest, also, more like... like blood. Dried blood. They shouted to each other, though, like men did after a hunt. Spirits were silent, so they were men after all, but not any kind of man Mokolo had ever seen before, with faces the color of old deerskin, or clouds, or red.

Datolo made a motion indicating that they were not going to go anywhere soon and they must stay quiet. His eyes were red and swimming about in his face, so Mokolo knew he was feeling fear and confusion, too. As they watched, the other men continued to skin the bear. Once that was finished, they began cutting off its legs and finally, two of them removed the bear's huge head, stacking everything up along the stream bank. Mokolo understood that much, but what happened next he could not understand. Other men rolled the rest of the bear into the stream, then sat together and began eating some of the bear's meat.

Why did they throw away the largest part of the bear? He couldn't imagine why, unless it was some kind of prayer offering. None of their hunters would waste that much of any kill. Meat was too precious, and the spirit of the life taken would be angry. It showed no respect for the bear at all.

He began to feel angry. Bears were enemies in the old days; but now, they kept to themselves as did the clan. *Why go out of your way to kill one and then dishonor it, too?* The other men must be very stupid or evil to do that. He wished he could ask Datolo if he knew, but he kept silent, watching. The Mother's helper crept up close and watched, with a grimace as the butchering continued.

It took a while, but the other men finally bound up the bear meat and the poor bear's head, lashing them to a long pole, while two of other men did the same with the skin. One of them, Mokolo saw, lifted a waterskin and drank from it. That also proved they were not spirits, but men. Some kind of men. They broke into pairs who took the poles bearing the bear meat, its head and severed paws upon their shoulders. The two pairs then strode off through the grass, while the remaining men gathered up bundles of small spears and three narrow sticks bent like half-hoops.

Datolo nudged Mokolo and pointed to the other man gathering up the bent sticks. He slung them over one shoulder. They were only a bit shorter than he was tall, so they hung down almost to the ground. With his other hand, he took a bundle of small spears as his fellows did the same. Mokolo saw no throwing sticks or even a single heavy spear. He looked at Datolo and saw he was deep in concentration. He watched the four remaining other men stride off, and saw how the bent sticks were held on by thin sinews or deerskin lacing tied to each end. The other men were talking their strange language so they could be heard long after they disappeared into the tall grass, but as they watched it part showing where the other men were heading.

Datolo motioned for the rest to follow. It took them a few minutes to gather up everything, but as they followed from above, soon, they saw the other men again, gathered below. One was pointing towards another patch of tall grass ahead of them.

Mokolo saw one of them put his finger in the air. Maybe they were checking the wind, just like he did. It was blowing from beyond the grass. The four put down their burdens, and other men unslung the sticks off their shoulders and passed them around so each man had a long bent stick. Next, they could see clearly, how each took one of the small spears… and... each small spear was put into the thin sinew cord at one end, and held by the man's hand against the bent stick on the other end. The men crouched down as proper hunters would, and their leader made a motion for them to spread out along the grass-line. Two, he motioned to enter first. They each held their bent sticks forward while they pulled back on the small spear attached to the sinew cord as they crept into the grass. Above, the three watchers followed the other men's movements, clearly from the way the grass parted, from their hidden position, and saw how some game animal had suddenly broken and was running fast, back towards the way the men had come. Mokolo thought it was a clever way to flush out game.

The rest of the other men followed fast behind, and when the fourlegs broke free of the tall grass, Mokolo saw two of the other men step out into the sunlight and hold up the bent sticks. They let go of the small spears together, and the small spears flew straight and very fast, into the four-leg's neck. It only took a moment. First, it sprung into the air and tried to run away, but after only a few steps it stumbled and the other men fell upon it with knives. The rest of the other men followed and a great shout went up. It made Mokolo shiver as the fear began climbing up his back again.

Mokolo watched Datolo slowly nodding as the hunt below ended. Datolo then motioned for all three of them to creep back up into the forest. Mokolo was glad. He didn't want to be stuck full of small spears, and he didn't want the other men to see him. He didn't like them. He didn't like their honey colored hair or their white faces or their bent sticks that threw the small spears faster than his eyes could follow. He wished he were back home at his clan's cave. He looked at the Mother's helper. Her name was Anas'kala. She was still only a young girl, but she had a grave job to do. She was also fighting back tears.

Chapter 14

"Anson," shouted Kells, bringing up the spent arrows and bows from the ground, "that was a stroke of luck!"

He was in the lead, carrying one end of the pole with the bear meat, and he called back to Kells. "A bear and a deer in one day is the best hunting luck I've ever had, but it was your arrow that found the bear."

"But it was your arrow that found the deer!" replied Kells, as he walked past taking over the lead spot.

Two hunters behind them began a cheerful hunting song. Everyone soon joined in. The words sung in time with their footfalls and the meat swung back and forth on its poles in accompaniment. The sound drifted up and along the Valley and found the three watchers crouching in the safety of the forest's cover. They stood, and began walking back towards their home and away from the other men and their hunt song.

As they sang, each man began thinking of what he would do with his share of the bear's claws. A successful bear hunt was a glorious thing and each would proudly wear a number of the animal's long, curving claws. Its head would be presented to the Seer, who would skin it, boil away the flesh and use the skull in rituals of healing, to give them more power. The meat would be shared with the whole village, especially those who were hurt or fighting illness. There was no medicine as powerful as bear meat and the hunters were proud to bring it home. Prouder still, was Anson, who was bringing back all of the hunters with no injuries or losses. He knew that Gudrun would be bragging about him to the other women for months.

As he began thinking of how his wife would repay his courage and sure skills, the hunter behind him, called his name quietly.

"Anson?"

"Lind? You've been a quiet one -- are you alright?"

Lind looked down at his feet. He wasn't alright. Something he saw when the bear was struck worried him. He didn't want to bring evil onto their hunt. The other hunters were happy and proud, but he had something to tell Anson. "I'm worried about something, Anson. You and I should walk a bit faster so the other men won't hear." He sped up his pace as did Anson.

"So what is the secret, Lind?"

"I saw them. Trolls. They were watching us from above… in the forest."

"You saw trolls?" Anson's face darkened and his brows drew in as he thought of the evil that even seeing a troll could bring. Now, if Lind was not just fancying things, trolls were watching their hunts.

"Are you sure."

Lind took a moment to think about what had happened. He had been following close behind Anson as they crept up on the bears, but he dropped his arrow as he began to nock it on the bowstring. He had to turn around and pick it up, and at that exact instant, he glanced up to the forest's edge and saw movement in the brush. Later, when they were butchering the bear, he glanced up and saw the shapes of two or three trolls, watching from above. When he looked again, they had disappeared, but he answered, "Yes, I'm sure I saw them."

Anson slowed his pace and said "Say nothing to the other men. I will decide what to tell Nils."

"Agreed." Said Lind.

The rest of the day's trek was mostly quiet, one of the hunters called out that an eagle was following them, but no songs were sung. They camped that night in a new shelter, under a rock overhang. They no longer used the place where Raaka died, for fear of the knife-lions who dwelt nearby. It was a quiet night, but cold. Anson decided to leave soon after first light. He told them they would not stalk more game. There were only five of them, and even one more deer, would be too heavy to bear quickly home.

And Anson wanted to be home as quickly as they could, or at least safely out of the valley. He puzzled over what Lind had seen. They were not attacked, only watched. It might mean the trolls were planning to follow them, but he had watched the forest closely as they travelled through the valley and saw nothing. He knew Lind was also keeping his eyes open. Still, he didn't want to bring trolls to his village. It was a bad omen to have even seen them. He thought that maybe it was the hunters' pride that had blinded them, all except Lind. He was glad Lind told him.

Nils approached them first, as they came down the last miles towards the village. Anson made the signal for them to slow and stop near the lake, where there were some boulders to place the meat poles across. The other hunters were glad to unburden their aching shoulders, and they all sat and chewed on some dried meat and berries, while Nils and Anson spoke quietly, away from them.

"Lind was sure? The sunlight can fool the eyes, sometimes," said Nils.

I know, especially when a hunter is afraid," replied Anson, adding, "but we were none of us afraid, we were happy and proud. None of us had a single dark thought."

Nils nodded, grasping his bearded chin in one hand. He closed his eyes and considered what should be done. The worst thing was, that these trolls seemed to travel during the light of day. He had always believed they were afraid of the sun. He looked up at the top of the hill closest to them, where the path coming from the valley ran between two large boulders. At the top of each one, deep brush piled against the wind. It was the one area, near the lake, clear of any forest trees or cover. If anyone approached, they would be seen a long distance away. He lay his hand on Anson's shoulder and pointed up towards the hill.

"We'll build a shelter up there, on this side of the rocks, that won't be seen from the other side."

Anson nodded, thinking about how many logs it might take as Nils continued his explanation. When Nils finished, Anson asked him, "It might work best with two – one on either side – do you agree?"

More than one man watching is better, but it would mean more work to build another shelter. "They must be strong and they must have walls, not just a roof."

Anson agreed and asked how big they should be and the discussion continued until they had agreed that each should be large enough to sleep two men, with a third man able to watch from above, from behind the very top of the boulder. Each would take turns at the top, while the other men slept or ate. But six men were needed, and it would be hard to decide which six men could leave their families and risk themselves. Nils clapped Anson on the back, saying, "Oh, by the way, you led another good hunt! We will all be thankful. Let's get that meat down to the village before the flies take it!"

Lind saw the chief approach. He had figured he'd have to talk with him, but the stern look in the chief's eyes as he stood made him wonder if it was going to be worse than that.

"As soon as you get the meat set up, understand?"

"Yes, Nils, I will come to find you as soon as we have finished." Lind replied, gravely.

Later, after leaving Nils' house he had time to consider everything. It turned out it was worse than he'd expected it to be. It turned out he'd have to speak with the Seer as well. The Seer had frightened him since he was a child. He didn't look forward to having to go anywhere near the strange, old hut the Seer lived in either. It gave him chills every time he passed it by.

Chapter 15

"Can you make a bent throwing stick, Mokolo?" The Clan Mother's eyes were hard and flinty.

He considered her question again, carefully, reaching up to scratch the sweaty wrapping over his eyes. "Yes, Mother, I am sure I can. I may have to make a few of them before it will work, though. It may take some time to get it right. Can your helper provide me with strong sinew cords as long as a man is tall?"

"She will have they them braided right away. You should start immediately. Your work is very important to the Clan. I don't have to tell you to pay attention to each thing you do?"

"No Mother, I will take the time to do it right."

"Then accept my blessings and the blessings of the Great Mother. We will speak again before the moon thins."

He heard her rise and shuffle out, then he felt her helper near. She told him he could remove the wrappings, which he did, keeping his eyes respectfully down. But he felt her touch on his arm. She was touching him! He looked up into a worried young face.

She whispered, "Can you do this?"

"Yes," he replied," Don't worry. It will be fine."

She thanked him, her hand resting on his arm, holding his gaze longer than it was necessary. He felt nervous, but also a little worried. What if someone saw them together like this? This close, he could see that she was more woman than little girl. She was just small in stature and slight, but he could see the swell of her breasts and the gleam in her eyes. Why was she doing this?

"I should… I should go now." he said.

"If you have need, go." She removed her hand, but her eyes held his a moment more. Then, as he rose, she spoke again, saying, "We will speak again. I have asked the Mother... asked her for you."

Really? He wondered. The idea thrilled him, but frightened him also. How would he keep his attention focused now? He turned to leave then turned back and asked her name.

"I am Anas'kala and you are Mokolo."

Later, as he sat staring at the pile of long saplings he'd asked for, he wondered how he would do this. He had a small pile of new, broad scraping blades with sharp, clear edges. He had spent time with Datolo and the two had drawn in the loose soil, how they remembered the bent sticks carried by the other men. He remembered them one way, Datolo another. He decided to combine both ways. He would scrape the sticks thin, from each end, but leave the centers full round, to fit the grip of the hand.

Grasping the nearest, he began pulling long strokes down, as curls of shredded bark and wood fell from the blade in his grip. A folded deerskin protected his palm. It took many strokes to thin the stick properly, but with each scrape he heard "Anas'kala" instead of the sound of the wood being thinned. It troubled him.

When the sun was full overhead, Baaktolo approached him with a basket of fresh berries and meat. He smiled and said, "I'll join you for a while. We can eat and talk a little. You've been so silent lately."

"I'm sorry... yes, please let me share your food" Mokolo lay the stick he was working on down, and he shifted his weight to turn towards Baaktolo who lay the basket between them.

"You didn't stop working all day yesterday. Aren't you tired or hungry?" His friend looked concerned for him.

"Yes, I'm tired and hungry, but this has to be done right. I'm still not sure if it will work, but I guess Datolo will say when I can stop." He took some berries and ate them greedily as Baaktolo did the same.

As they ate, they spoke of small matters, the next hunt, the cold nights. As the basket emptied, Baaktolo moved closer and said quietly, "Are you sure it's just your work that has your mouth closed?"

"What do you *mean*?" replied Mokolo, a bit more defensively than he had wished.

"Someone whose name I forget... mentioned that he heard two Lesser Mothers speaking. Your name was mentioned."

"What does that mean? Women talk all the time?"

"Well... your name was mentioned, then he heard the word "chosen". Have you been given to a woman without telling me?" Baaktolo's eyes gleamed and he licked his lower lip in a way that made his friend cringe away slightly.

"I... I... I don't know for sure. I can't really say. We shouldn't be speaking about it anyway!" He looked left and right to be sure no one was listening, then added, "But maybe. I'm having enough trouble focusing on my work without this. Promise me you won't speak of this to anyone else. Promise." He glared sternly at his friend's goofy expression and bugged-out eyes.

"Alright. I promise I won't speak of your being chosen to anyone else. But, surely you can tell me who she is?"

"Quiet!" Mokolo hissed, "Do you want to bring shame on me?" When his friend shook his head, he said, "Her name is Anas'kala. She is the Clan Mother's helper and daughter of her daughter."

Baaktolo became agitated hearing her station. He rose with the basket, and hurried away to sit on the other side of the clearing. From time to time, Mokolo thought he heard him giggling, but each time he glanced over at him, Baaktolo was looking away.

Before the sun slipped down behind the ridge line, the two friends and Datolo had already tied sinew cords to the sticks pulling them into a bent position approximating what they had seen, then tying them off on the free end. It wasn't going well. Each was worse than the next, and the sinews did not end straight on both ends, but Datolo said it would have to do for now.

He had brought a pile of the small spears that Mokolo had made, and he picked up the first, put it against the sinew cord and the middle of the bent stick, as he had seen, then raised the stick up. He pointed the small spear towards a large tree several man-lengths away and let go of the small spear.

It fell weakly to the ground where he stood. He tried it again, and the same thing happened. Then he tried flinging the stick like a throwing stick, but that didn't work.

He asked Baaktolo what he thought, and Baaktolo picked up one of the completed bent sticks and held it out. He sighted along the sinew cord, holding the stick level with the ground. At least the cord was very straight. When he pulled on its center, it resisted and the stick bent more. He tried this several times, then, without a small spear, he released the middle of the sinew and it made a thronging noise as the bent stick returned to the shape it was before.

He looked at Datolo to see the older man smiling broadly. "That is it!" Datolo exclaimed.

"What?" asked Mokolo.

"Just watch", said Datolo, standing and picking up another small spear. This time, once the cord was aligned with the notch in the end of the small spear, he let the other end rest loosely on top of his fist gripping the bent stick. He pulled the cord back, in the middle, while holding the small spear at its end and when it was pulled back very tight, he released the small spear.

IT FLEW! It flew fast and long, but not where he wanted it to go. Off to the side, they heard it finally come down in some bushes, and Mokolo grinned. "It flew!" he said.

"You made it fly!" Baaktolo added.

"No," said Datolo, "Not me. The cord and the stick threw it. First it was tight, then it released power into the small spear when I let it go. Here, try it yourselves."

The next few days, the men took turns learning to shoot the arrows fast, if not always where they wanted them to go. It was Datolo that learned to raise a finger up and over, to hold the arrow close to the wood stick as it was let go. The feathers would just slip through. That gave them more accuracy. By the evening of the third day, both men could put the arrow into whatever tree they wanted it to fly to. Some of the bent sticks worked better than other men, some just cracked and broke in two when the cord was pulled back. Some were strong enough to withstand the intense bending. Mokolo remembered which trees had given those saplings and branches. He made more, some thinner, some thicker.

Sometimes, if they didn't pull the small spear back far enough, it would just bounce off the tree, but when they pulled it back far until they could barely hold it, the arrow flew fast and bit deep into the tree. The tree looked like it had sprouted a tangle of straight, small branches. Datolo thought it was time they showed the Clan Mother what they had learned. They all gathered up the bent sticks that remained and the loose small spears, and walked back to the cave path with smiles on their faces.

Chapter 16

"You have done well." The Clan Mother's deep voice almost sounded soft and soothing. Three men sat, their eyes wrapped, their bows across their legs. She directed the next question to Mokolo.

"How soon can you make enough for all our hunters? Three hands and two."

He counted the time, and then counted the trees he'd need to pull branches from, then replied, "Before the next turning of the moon, but I will need twice that number of sinew cords. They break after many uses."

"That will be good. I will make sure the cords are made ready for you, but before I give you my blessing, I must see this for myself."

Both men drew in their breath quickly. How could that happen? The Clan Mother never left the cave. She usually was never seen beyond the woman's rooms, unless someone was to be laid to rest, and then she was masked from sight. Datolo spoke with great care. Mokolo winced as he heard the words.

"But how would you see us using the bent sticks? Our eyes must be bound, and you must remain within the cave's protection?"

They heard a deep, rumbling laugh which filled the small side-passage. Both men relaxed slightly. They must not have angered her. They waited as her laughter lessened and she said, "Why, you... you will show me, here, of course!" She called for Anas'kala, who knelt before her as the Mother explained what would be done, then she carefully removed the wrappings around each man's eyes. The two men were speechless. They stared at the ground out of their fear and deep respect. Finally the Clan Mother spoke.

"This has been blessed by the Great Mother, who teaches us that proper respect may be withheld if a moment of importance arrives and the Clan must be protected, so… raise up your eyes and look into the face of your Mother with no fear."

Anas'kala had returned with a burning brand which lit up the inside of the passage brightly. Slowly, each man lifted his eyes up into the beaming, smiling face of the ancient Clan Mother. Her face was deeply lined, as lined as the very rocks and the bark of the biggest trees… but it was kind. Her eyes were as black as the darkest night, but somehow, they sparkled. She quickly explained to them that she would stand behind them and they would shoot the small spears deep into the passage, where a large food basket has been placed in a niche in the rock.

"You will try to send your small spears to pierce the basket. Can you do that?"

The both said "Yes, Mother." And for the next few hours, their target skills improved as both Anas'kala and the Clan Mother clapped and laughed each time the basket was pierced. Finally, they had used up all the small spears they had brought, and she bade them sit, while she lay her hands on both men's shoulders, one at a time blessing them and thanking them, from the depths of her heart, for figuring out how the other men could kill from a distance.

She ended by saying, "We were always told to flee from strangers and danger. When the other men first came, my lesser mother's mother told her to shun them, and never let them see us. Now I understand that we should have at least watched them and learned from them. If we have their fast-flying small spears, we will not need to fear them, and you two have given that to us."

Mokolo still felt his heart would burst with the pride he carried for days after. He worked with Baaktolo and selected the very best straight branches from the short trees that were green all winter. Their red wood was stronger and more flexible than most of the other men. He made each bow about the same height as a man stood, leaving off two hand widths so men could run with their bows slung over their shoulders as he had seen. During that week, the large water birds returned, so there were many feathers to use and everyone's belly was full. Mokolo found that if the cords were tied into small loops at each end and the bent sticks notched at each end, a man could take off an old cord and put on a new one very quickly. They also found that the bent sticks stayed stronger if they were unstrung so they could straighten between uses. It was a very happy time. A time of great learning. Mokolo wondered why what now seemed so simple to him had been hidden from his people for so long.

The stone workers who shaped knives and scrapers now had to make many tiny knives for the small spears. It took longer, and they grumbled a bit until Datolo brought them to the clearing and showed them what their tiny knives were being used for. After that, they made them so fast the two friends couldn't keep up with small spears. By the time the moon turned, they had presented each hunter with a bent stick, several cords and a handful of small spears, a tiny knife sparkling in the sun on the end of each one.

It was a hand of days later, that the old Fire Master, Tik'olo approached Mokolo and asked him to make him a small bent stick.

"About as long as my arm… and can you make me a hand of small spears with no feathers and no knife on the end, just two plain ends?"

"Of course, but why would you want that?"

Tik'olo just smiled and said, "You're not the only one who has ideas. I'll show you when I'm ready."

By the time Tik'olo had showed Datolo and Mokolo what he had used the small bent stick for, sending cheers and laughs up into the night air, one of the stone workers had thought it might be a good idea if they tried putting knives on the ends of their spears, too; not just burning them to a sharp, black point. He had tried to pull some of Datolo's practice arrows from a tree and they were stubborn. They wouldn't let go. He knew that spears often did not bite deeply and the prey could shake them loose. If his idea worked, the knives would help the spears stay in and bite deeper.

This was tried the very next hunt, and it worked well. They needed fewer spears to bring down the fourlegs. The Clan Mother was very pleased, but still she resisted using the bent sticks and small spears on a hunt. She also told Datolo to only hunt the upper parts of the valley, not down towards where they had made contact with the unknown men.

"Keep your party close. It will protect us to stay silent, too, when you hunt and bring back meat."

Datolo recognized her concerns, and it was so. Their hunts became more efficient. As summer ran its course, they traveled shorter distances and almost always brought back all the fourlegs they could carry. Until the winter came their bellies were always full. But then, the winter came and the fourlegs who had been so plentiful during the long days, began to move away down the valley.

Chapter 17

Anson tried to find a comfortable position for his
shoulders at the corner made inside the log palisade where
he spent his watch. His other watch mates lay below,
within the small, log house. Sleeping, he thought. Anson's
watch on the roof of the small guardhouse, would be
finished at first light. He knew it wasn't too far off, but
each twist and turn he made, made him less comfortable
than the one before.

After a long deliberation, at the end of summer, Nils
had made the final decision to build the outpost, at the top
of a small knoll on the approach path near the lake. The
village was not so far that beating the hollow log
suspended upon the roof wouldn't be heard. During the
day, when people were working and walking and visiting,
it could be heard easily, but after nightfall... he wondered
if it was loud enough to wake them. To warn them.

Anson rubbed his weary eyes and tried to focus them
to penetrate the darkness. The moon had gone down some
time before, and while the dawn was coming, the
remaining time left Anson in almost complete darkness.
On nights when the clouds were overhead, there weren't
even sparks of starlight to help him watch the ridges and
passes approaching the lake.

While he stared into blackness, he worried about
Gunda. She'd taken ill before, but this time, she hadn't
grown strong after a few days. The healers' herbs and
even the Seer could not find a reason. There was always a
reason for illness. Everyone said so. But this time... he
was losing his faith in the knowledge of the wise, and here
he was... sitting in the cold on a hard wooden roof instead
of helping with his daughter, home where he belonged.

He rubbed the back of his neck and turned his head
towards the East. There it was, a faint glow was rising

over the ridges. Finally! He picked up the heavy staff by his side and holding it vertically, thumped it hard upon the lapped plank surface of the roof a few times until the angry sound of someone's voice called up to him from the smokehole – "Enough! We're roused!"

After the usual sleepy greeting from the new watcher, Anson climbed the ladder down to the ground and rapped on the heavy locked door. He heard the big wood slide moving and pushed the door open as soon as it started to move.

The other man remaining in the watch house, was tending the fire, to heat some water and bake some acorn loaves. Anson saw no meat, so he grumbled a morning blessing and slunk off to his bed, waiting in the shadows.

"Do you want to eat first?"

No. I want to sleep first." He settled the bearskin around his shoulders and found a comfortable spot for his head to rest. Before sleep came, he found himself thinking about what he could do to help his daughter regain her health. There were no more answers and it made him feel useless and weak.

Chapter 18

Towards evening, a sharp rap on the door woke him. He wiped his eyes, coughing from the smoke of the fire, then pushed off the bearskin and rose, holding onto the log wall for balance. The new watchers had come from the village. It was time to return. He knocked against the ceiling with a long pole near the door, and bade the replacements enter. The second man, who'd been cutting wood, returned also, with a load for the fire-pit. After dumping it into the space, he began gathering up his few possessions as Anson spoke about what had passed through the night.

"Nothing. No one at all… except the scream of a cat, off somewhere towards the end of the lake, but that happens almost every night anyway. None of us saw any fires, but you may want to ask Lars, when he comes down, yourself."

He shook the watch leader's hand, and gathered his bag heading for the door. The firelight danced on the shiny surface of the log walls, and it caught his eye before he pulled the heavy door open, passed outside and headed home. Lars was just coming around the side of the palisade.

"See anything?"

"Besides an occasional star? Nope. Nothing. Oh! I heard a fish jump." He nodded as he passed, to get his kit.

Anson usually enjoyed the long walk home. It ran downhill for most of the way, and the shoreline was always his favorite place to just sit and think. Just the same, today, he found it longer than normal. His staff swung with each step, but it didn't help him get home any faster. His thoughts were with his daughter. He wanted to hear how her nights had been and if there was any change the past few days. He didn't notice the polished loop of root that had waited for every traveler on this path for as long as it had been a path. It caught his foot and he went down, face-first.

"Bear's Balls!" He shouted. His nose had taken the full impact, and was now sitting less than straight on his face. Blood ran into his beard already full of pine needles and sticks. He used one to scrape the dirt off his teeth.

Anson pulled himself together and found a rock to sit on alongside the trail, waiting to stand and resume his walk home. After a few moments, he heard one of his watch mates coming up behind him, and ashamed he'd been so pre-occupied he'd missed the root, he hid his face.

"Anson! You're all bloody! What happened?"

"He peeked out over his hand and replied, "Nothing. I'm fine."

"Hold on – you don't look fine. Let me take a look." The man reached for Anson's hand, pulling it away from his face and added, "Ohhh. That's not the way your nose looked when you left. It's really… crooked. It has to be set. I can do it for you."

"Alright, if you think it shouldn't wait…"

There was a sharp crack as the other man grabbed it and pulled it straight down. "Hey, why didn't you warn me? That hurt like a kick in the balls."

"Sorry. Had to be done, and I didn't want you to struggle. It's much… better now. You should go down to the lake and wash up your face and beard. Your wife will be terrified. It looks like you had a fight with a small bear… instead of a terrible root!" He walked off laughing as Anson got up and slid down to the rocky shoreline.

He found a flat stone to kneel on, and bent over, cupping his hands together. The water from the lake was icy cold, and the blood ran from his hands and face in small pink streams which drifted away on the light current. It seemed to attract a few small fish, which swam excitedly into the murky pinkness. As he was in no mood to watch fish, he picked up a rock and sent them scurrying away as he tossed it in where they had grouped up. "Bear's Balls." He muttered, then began to chuckle at himself. He sat there, laughing softly for a few moments longer, as the second of his watch mates passed quickly, wondering what the joke was.

The ripples cleared and the water again smoothed out. He looked across at the far shore, and the wavelets rippled like silver, all the trees growing upside down into the depths of the lake. He brought his gaze back, closer, then up towards the far end of the lake, where the small river fell in with a short, noisy fall and hazy run. He couldn't see the cattails that grew there, but he could just make out the top of the falls, and... what was that? Despite the distance, he thought he'd seen a large, dark animal moving across the open mouth of the river, but it wasn't a bear... unless... He watched, trying to focus his eyes better, but the fall's haze obscured the details.

There! Once again, he saw a shape move across the top of the falls. Then another one. After waiting several more moments, and once he was sure no other men moved in the distance, he rose and returned to the watch house, to report what he'd seen. He wasn't exactly sure, but even if it was a group of bears, they should know. He'd also have to tell Nils what he'd seen. It filled his already heavy heart with leaden worry. He knew he wouldn't be home until after darkness had fallen.

Chapter 19

"…but you're not sure, are you?"

"No. I'm not sure, but whatever I saw on the falls was… was walking on two legs, not four." Anson knew Nils had a right to caution. He knew the time away from the hunt and harvest had left the village already a tiny bit weaker for facing winter. He knew. Anson just wished he could be certain that he'd seen bears, or deer, or even the big wolves that hadn't been seen for many years now. Even people.. anything but trolls.

Nils walked back and forth across the floor, pulling on his beard. Anson waited, as he had before. Nils' eyes were on the floor as he paced, then he stopped right in front of where Anson sat.

"It was still daylight, was it not? That proves it wasn't trolls, doesn't it?"

"Well, we thought they only travelled after dark, until… until the hunt in the valley proved us wrong. But it might have been men, too. Unknown men. Either way, it's not good. Threats can come from lots of directions at once, it…"

Nils cut him off, with a quick, angry gesture. "Don't tell me about threats. I've taken us through threats before - - even through hard fights, or have you forgotten the bears at the mouth of the high valley?"

"No, of course not. I'm just worried for my family. For all our families. I worried when we first took the hunt up into the high valley. I hope we haven't awakened *any* kind of threat, but I know that we'll face it and protect ourselves the best we can."

"That's right… the best we can." Nils lay a hand on Anson's shoulder. "The game always moves on, and we can't survive without a source of meat, especially when the lake freezes up. Do you remember my saying that?"

"Yes. It was when I came to talk about the stories of the high valley and trolls... and my fears."

Nils lay his other hands on the other shoulder. "And after we spoke, I spent time with the Seer. You remember. It took three days and three nights, but he told us that the valley held no danger for us."

Anson nodded, but his face remained dark, his brows knit tightly. "But they were there, weren't they? Trolls. Now maybe they have come down to the falls. Will it take them coming and breaking down our gates before we understand they mean us no good? How did the Seer's visions fail us?"

"No. You are right. We need to do something. I just want to remind you that all those moons back, when you saw them, none of us were actually hurt, were they? I believe the Seer has power to protect our hunts and our village, from the likes of trolls. Still, maybe we should send out three or four armed hunters to see what they can find out... will you find three or four willing to venture back up there?"

"I'll lead them myself!" replied Anson, rising to his feet, but Nils patted his shoulders and pressed him back down.

"Not so fast. You will stay here. The village needs you to lead as many hunts as we can manage before the snow flies off the mountains and the lake freezes. We need to dry more meat while we still get sun during the day. You'll have to find someone else."

Anson felt torn in half. Part of him wanted to remain home to do exactly what Nils said, and spend more time with his family... with Gunda. But, of course, he knew that unless he led them, it would be very hard to find anyone willing to leave at this time of year... especially to walk right into the hands of enemies.

"Can you do that Anson? Can you find a group to search for our new enemies?"

"Yes, Nils. I'll do my best."

"We know you will, Anson." Nils stepped back, and Anson clapped his chest as he rose. When he stepped out of Nils' door, the moon had risen, laying a soft, silver light over the houses, the trees and the lake. He thought everything looked so peaceful as the light of fires beginning to shine through open doors and windows. He turned towards his home, thinking that the way things looked was not always the way they really were.

Chapter 20

Below them, the lake's gleaming waters spread out into the dark distance. In it, the moon and the stars were reflected in a full, mirror image. Few ripples disturbed it as the wind was very light. Mokolo pulled his heavy bearskin around his shoulders to keep as warm as he could. There would be no fire. Datolo had made it clear that they must be unseen. The Clan Mother herself had given Datolo very specific instructions. Anas'kala also sat silently, wrapped in her bearskin, watching out. So close, he felt her pressing into his back. Baaktolo was also with them, leaning up against a crown of roots surrounding the base of the huge tree where they had taken shelter for the night. It stood very close to the edge of the river, as it fell over the rocks on its way to the lake.

Datolo returned to the three of them who were waiting. He made no noise as he moved and tapped each of them, pointing out to the lake. Far, far out along the lake… in the distance, the light of many fires could be seen, glowing warm yellow dots in the darkness. They couldn't see the people who made those fires burn, but there were many fires. Many other people. Many new enemies.

The tree, beneath which they sat, was very tall, with huge, spreading branches. Datolo pointed up, with both hands repeatedly. Mokolo was uncomfortable enough on the ground, especially with a young girl so close he could feel her pressing against him. He tried not to acknowledge the warm excitement he felt spreading inside. each time she moved. Now Datolo wanted them to climb the tree. It was the only thing they could do to remain safe after dark, with no fire, so he rose to comply.

Ana'skala beat them all to her feet and began climbing quickly until she was lost to their sight. Finally, they rest joined the climb, finding her wedged up so high in the tree's branches, no one or nothing could follow her. Only her feet hung down below the dark mass of her burdens and her bearskin to show them she was with them. Mokolo was not happy she was along, but at least it wasn't the Clan Mother herself, accompanying them. Datolo told him he had found the courage somewhere, to argue that the clan needed her to remain behind. She grudgingly, it seemed to Mokolo, sent her grand-daughter as the girl was strong with the sight and could hear the spirits' lessons, and not so old and slow. They had still taken four full days to reach the falls. There had been little discussion, as the Mother had told them each to remain as silent as possible and leave no trace of their passing. It made for slow travel.

Mokolo waited until the other men had found secure places to pass the night, then he wedged himself in as tightly in a deep cleft in the bark as he could, and found a piece of dried meat and some nuts. A meager meal, but better than nothing at all. As he chewed, he looked out, through the branches and remaining leaves, to the shining lake, and the firefly-sized dots of fire. Tomorrow, when the darkness came, they would be close enough to see how these enemies lived and what kind of men they were. He unwrapped the braided skin belt he wore around his waist and tied himself, his bag of small feathered spears, his full spear with the stone knife bound to the end and his bent, strung stick into the branches so if he slept nothing would fall. He knew it would be a sleepless night, though as little comfort was found high in a tree, except for birds. As he gazed out into the darkness, he thought he heard the girl far above him, singing the sacred life song, very quietly... but he wasn't sure if it was just the wind in the branches after all.

# # # #

The next day, once they were all safely back on the ground, Datolo wanted an early departure. They were a good distance north of the falls, where the cliff broke down into a series of deep gorges and broken rock falls, so they followed one down through heavy brush. No game trails to follow on this floor, and the going was slow. It was midday before the four of them gathered at the edge of a flat, grassy plain. It led gently downhill to the lake, but there was little cover to hide them, so Datolo called a rest and a meal while he decided which way to continue.

Anas'kala sat under a small tree, apart from the rest of them. While Mokolo chewed his dried meat he saw her lips moving and realized she was singing silently. He looked away in embarrassment. It wouldn't do for him to watch her making ceremony. That was only for the Lesser Mothers and the Clan Mother. Datolo walked away, under what cover he could find along the edge of the remaining trees, until he disappeared from sight. Mokolo was worried. These were not the Clan's hunting lands. Anything could be lurking up ahead, and without the wisdom of Datolo, they would be lost.

He returned, laying his finger over his mouth. He motioned for them to retreat into the deeper brush, and they followed, silently, until they were back behind the last of the fallen rock. He then gathered them close and spoke in a whisper.

"I've been up along the edge of the trees until I saw an open rock outcropping that would allow us to watch the enemies from above. The approach is well hidden, from below, but I believe we can climb up across this slope, easily." He gestured diagonally over and up pointing at the top, before continuing, "from there, we can walk to the high, flat place, and crawl to its edge to see what we may see, once night comes." He looked into each face, to see understanding, then added, "There is a hunting party of six men – tall men, not tiny ones – approaching through the grass. We must move quickly and silently." The three nodded and quietly patted their chests, signifying their understanding.

Mokolo packed up his kit and got ready to follow Datolo. He felt his excitement rise, but also fear... and anger. The men who killed his father were coming. He wished he could strike them with his spear and kill them all, but when Datolo motioned, he fell in at the end of the four, quietly.

It wasn't an easy climb, over a talus slope of broken rock with only the occasional growth of brush to hide them from below. Their direction took them, at one point up above the tops of the trees below. Datolo motioned a halt, and sent them, one at a time, up to the next cover. At least they were very near the top now, and the rest of the journey to the watching place would be an easy walk, well-concealed.

A sudden cry of a bird alerted them to what might well be the other men hunting below. Mokolo drew in his breath, and they all waited a moment. There was a muffled crack as a rock fell and skidded down a slope, but no other sound followed. A few moments later, as they resumed their journey, they heard another muffled crack, but this time from further away. Mokolo let his breath out. So far, they were sure they had not been seen.

# # # #

As they walked down along a game trail that skirted the top- edge of the slope, Mokolo relaxed a bit. The travel was easy – the tall, dark pines left a soft cushion of spent needles under foot, so they moved silently and smoothly. Through a break in the trees up ahead, Mokolo saw the watching place getting nearer. It was a large, flat rock that thrust out through the forest and hung over the slope below. It was a natural place from which to see

everything that was going on below. Perfect for their
needs. Soon they would know how dangerous these new
men were. The watching place was close enough to the
men's camp that the smoke of their fires could be smelled
as it drifted up through the trees. It made Mokolo's eyes
smart and tear as much as each step forward weighed a
little heavier on his heart.

They were about to cross an area of sparse brush
cover, so they all crept down, closer to the ground when
suddenly, Datolo, in the lead, raised his hand and lowered
it quickly. They each dropped to the ground behind
whatever cover was there. Mokolo saw a small rock ledge,
and he stuffed himself under it, peering out through a
small cleft in the broken stone rubble. He heard a soft
noise approaching, rocks scattering. Maybe a knife-tooth
cat, or... he drew in his breath. A shaggy, huge, round
head with antlers rose above the edge of the slope and into
view. The rough noise rose and fell, then grew louder.
The sound became clearer. A gruff voice chanting
odd noises over and over. One of the other men, not an
animal. The head was covered by an elaborate fur and
feather hood with antlers attached to the crown. The
wearer's face was almost obscured by a heavy grey beard
that fell across his naked chest, where it tangled into a
variety of small animal skulls strung like a necklace. They
clacked and knocked together as he bounced over the
rough trail, in an odd gait, up to the top. Finally, his legs
and feet, all wrapped in fur, could be seen above the crest,
and Mokolo could finally see the entire man.
Short, but not small. He was quite fat, leaning heavily
on a thick wooden staff with the skull of a bear lashed to
its top end. There was a heavy bag slung over one
shoulder with green grass falling out of the open top. He
also carried a large water gourd and a big knife stuck into
a cord wrapped around his ample waist, but... no spear,

large or small. The dead bear's teeth gleamed as the sun struck them before the man turned along the same game trail and continued, walking away from them, bobbing from side to side, slowly, in the way of a very old person. Mokolo saw that he was heading towards the same place they were heading. He was filled with fear. What would Datolo do now?

The odd, old man disappeared around a bend in the trail that dipped into a well-shaded dell. Mokolo waited. The sun moved further behind them and the shadows were growing much longer when Datolo finally found him. Silently indicating for him to crawl out, Datolo gestured the shape of a large tree and climbing. So it was to be another night tied to branches high above the ground, trying to keep from watching Anas'kala. The four, re-joined in their journey kept silent as they glided between trees and back down to the game trail. Datolo motioned for them to leave the trail once they had passed up the other side of the brush-filled dell. They saw how the trail forked in the growing darkness, and they took the branch that led uphill, away from the edge of the slope and the watching place. Mokolo wondered which fork the old man had taken and how they would get to the watching place if he was there already. He listened for the chanting, but heard only a far-off bird call.

Chapter 21

The sun painted the sleeping form in the branches
with dappled light as it burned through the early fog.
Mokolo wrinkled his nose as he awoke, to dispel some
kind of bug which was working its way up his nostril. He
had to stifle a sneeze, then tried blowing it out. Far below,
Datolo heard him and glared up at him through the
branches, with the ever-present finger across his lips.
Mokolo saw him and nodded, then Datolo motioned out
from the tree and pointed. An opening between branches
revealed the watching rock and the floor of the valley
below. Mokolo was surprised. He hadn't thought the tree
had been that close to the edge, as they crept up to it in the
darkness. He also noticed a thin tendril of smoke rising
from the other side of a large group of boulders near to the
edge of the forest, lying upon the flat watch rock itself.

Datolo again made the silence sign, and motioned
Mokolo down to the ground. The rest were already
gathered behind the tree. Knowing that Anas'kala had
climbed down over his sleeping form without waking him,
made him blush and feel very foolish.

In a few moments, he joined them. The only sounds
he heard were a far-away bird singing a happy morning
song… and something else. The old man was chanting in
a low, puffing voice. The regular noises must have
awakened Datolo, who usually got little sleep during a
hunt. This, Mokolo knew, was a hunt as well. Maybe the
most important hunt he'd ever taken part in. Anas'kala
had again withdrawn to a brushy area and he saw her
mouth form silent words. As he looked away, Datolo and
Baaktolo both motioned him to join them. In a group, they
crept away from the tree and down a small cleft in the
forest floor, towards the edge of the slope until, Datolo
pointed through a natural weir of brush, to the watch rock.

They now had drawn up even with the old man and his fire.

Mokolo saw a rough shelter, formed by the space between the boulders, that had been used for some time. Chinks between the rocks had been filled with smaller rocks, and a ring of antlers, bleached by the sun lay amidst a ring of larger stones, spreading out from the opening in the rocks. In the center of these circles sat the old man, singing to his fire. As they were downwind, they caught the smell of the smoke, tearing their eyes. It was a sharp, disagreeable smell. Across the fire from the old man lay an empty bearskin within a ring of recently cut pine boughs. As the old man sang in his rough voice, Mokolo heard what sounded like an eagle answering the song. It repeated, then Mokolo saw a very large prey bird rise from behind the overhang, to hover above the edge of the watch rock. *Had the old man called the eagle?*

Datolo was completely focused upon the old man and the bird, which remained, hovering. Baaktolo and Mokolo also watched intently. Neither were aware as Anas'kala crept up from behind to join them. The only sound was her sharp breath when she saw the old man and the eagle hovering above him. The four remained in their hidden place, to see what was going to happen. For a long time, nothing happened, except that the bird finally flew off with the breeze, leaving a final sharp cry as a farewell.

The old man continued to sing, his hands upon his knees, until mid-day, when the sun flooded the rock with hard light. He stopped his song, and reached for his burden sack, which lay nearby, along with a few pieces of dry wood and his necklace of skulls. He began laying out different kinds of plants, some dry, some freshly cut, in piles between himself and the fire. The four, still unseen, watched as he raised his staff. Then using it, he slowly raised himself up on very unsteady feet. He then called out to the sky in a loud voice, then turned towards them and did the same, then turned his back to them and cried out again, then turned directly to the forest and called one last time. He remained standing still for a while, then slowly, settled back down using the staff for support, to a seating position on the rock itself. Mokolo wondered why he didn't sit upon the bearskin. *It had to be more comfortable.* Then he realized they were watching some kind of ritual, and almost felt he should look away.

As they watched, a new voice called up from beyond the edge of the watch rock. It repeated and the old man responded in like manner. The other man's voice called out and spoke for a time. Finally, the other man's head and body rose above the edge. He was burdened. A large bundle lay upon a frame made of branches, suspended from his shoulders on widely set, heavy hide straps. The bundle moved. He was bringing up an animal... no. A small arm appeared through the deerskin wrapping. Its hand grasped one of the stubs of the frame and held on tight. A small voice coughed raggedly, then asked something of the man carrying the burden. He responded, quietly, in a soothing tone. Another few coughs and the bundle was again quiet.

The man was tall, with honey colored hair and beard falling to his shoulders and chest. He was dressed in deerskin with a splash of cannily-sewn decoration on his chest that caught the sunlight. In one hand a spear, tipped with a knife served as a staff. But in the other hand, he clutched a bent, strung stick and some of the short, deadly spears with feathered shafts. He was a hunter. A very large knife hung suspended from his neck. It bobbed side to side, slinging against his chest with each heavy step. His face bore an expression like stone, his eyes set deep. He was not tiny. This was a man to be feared. He might, Mokolo thought, even be among the ones who killed his father.

Mokolo watched the man climb through a narrow cleft in the watch rock so slowly, so carefully that in Mokolo's mind, there could be no doubt that he bore upon his back, his own child. But why would he risk a long climb through the forest, from his camp nestled near the lake below? What could he find up here that was worth the risk to his child?

The old man shouted out some kind of guttural greeting, and the man with the burden replied, then he walked over close to the ring of stones and antlers and knelt down, removing his burden, very carefully while the old man began to sing again. As the old man sang, the hunter unwrapped the burden, now lying on the watch rock. He withdrew a braided deerskin cord, then began opening it up. The face of a young girl pushed out, sucked in a ragged, breath then coughed, with a phlegmy rattle. He knelt over her, and muttered a few words. She nodded, then the hunter bent his face down so low Mokolo wonder what he was saying to the child. He couldn't really see because the hunter's back was turned to them.

Her small, thin, arms, the color of old snow wrapped around the hunter's neck and he rose, carrying her across the ring of stones and antlers, to the empty bearskin near the fire, where he knelt upon the pine boughs and gently set her down. She wore only a light deerskin shirt that barely clung to her bony shoulders. Her hair, thin and also the color of honey, fell down her back and settled around her as she sat facing the fire. Each time the breeze blew, it lifted bits of her hair up, around her face. Her eyes, Mokolo saw, were very bright. Too bright. She was too thin and looked weak. She had an ugly cough. He thought he knew why she had been brought all the way up here. She was very ill. The old man must be a healer.

As he watched, he felt a hand upon his shoulder and looked up. Anas'kala stood behind him, her right hand rested upon his right shoulder, while the other one gripped the necklace of baby teeth she always wore. He knew not to speak to her, but one look and he was sure she was thinking the same thing. Could an old fat man help the hunter's daughter? Had they no Mother Healers?

Chapter 22

Anson sat beyond the Seer's stone ring, his eyes red
from lack of sleep. He tried to send his hope upwards, but
he couldn't take his eyes off Gunda. She sat still, unless
coughing... waiting for a cure, or even a little relief. He
saw her stick-thin legs and arms and wondered how much
longer she could wait. His oldest daughter, she now
weighed far less in his arms than the baby.

The Seer leaned over and withdrew several handfuls
of herbs and grasses from his small piles, then sprinkled
them over the small smoky fire. The skulls strung around
his neck made clattering noises as they hit together and
the sound made Anson wary. The sudden plumes of
smoke made Gunda cough. Anson had sworn to Gudrun
that he would bring a healthy child back to her, but... he
knew he should trust the wisdom of their Seer, but right
now, he didn't feel too hopeful.

The Seer reached across the smoke with a water
gourd and Gunda took it and drank.

"Finish it all, girl. Don't stop drinking until it's
gone." The Seer lay his hand gently on the girl's back.

She made a face that told her father it must have been
very bitter. The Seer nodded, then motioned for her to lie
down. Gunda lay back and straightened her legs as the
breeze again mingled the smoke with her hair, blowing
both around her face. She looked up at the sky. Cloudless,
all blue. Empty.

As the herb in the water the Seer had given her took
hold, her eyelids dropped, then she fell fast asleep. Anson
smiled a thin smile. It was the first sleep she'd had in
several days. He raised his eyes to the sky and sent out a
silent cry to the spirits for help. *How could they ignore her
pain?* She was so helpless. Anson's hands became fists,
knotted under his folded legs. The Seer again began to

sing his monotonous song calling down help from wherever the spirits dwelt.

As the Seer sang, Anson heard a far-off cry of a predatory bird. Soon a large hawk appeared from over the lake, drawing closer to them. Anson saw it coming, and hoped that it was a good sign. As the hawk glided nearer, playing on the updrafts, the Seer rose slowly gripping his staff, and began to hop and shuffle around the ring of stones. Anson moved back a few feet to give him more room. After he had circled three times, he retrieved his bundle and withdrew four sets of dried dewclaws, which he placed gently around his patient. One set above Gunda's head, then the second he ripped apart, laying a shriveled dewclaw near each of her elbows. The final two pair, also torn, were placed at her knees and below her feet. He returned to his place behind the fire, never missing even a single word in his song.

Anson looked around to find the hawk's silhouette above them, but it had gone. His stomach growled, but he knew none of them could eat during the ritual. He hoped the Seer didn't hear. Gunda lay still, apparently sleeping deeply. Only an occasional cough shook her now. He hoped he'd see some change transform her, but so far there was nothing to show for all their combined efforts.

# # # #

The day passed slowly. Only the breeze and the occasional bird call or shadow on the rock reminded any of them that time was passing. The Seer sang in his rough, croaking voice without a break in the monotonous cadence. Mokolo and his clan members waited, quietly watching from their hidden spot in the woods as the sun passed over and off towards their valley. Someone jostled Mokolo. It was Datolo. He motioned them all up and back into the forest, away from the place they'd been hiding.

They moved silently. Not a snapping twig or rolling stone alerted any living thing of their passage. They met the remains of the talus slope far within the woods, then skirted it, moving parallel to the valley, now far below them. With the crags far at their backs, now, they felt less worried about what they might find. When Datolo felt they could speak quietly together, he motioned them to rest ahead, under the spreading branches of a huge cedar. The bed of needles below was soft and aromatic.

Datolo first spoke. "Now we know they are only men. Not monsters, not tiny, but other men. They have strong weapons, but unless they have great power, they can be resisted. What say you, Helper to the Clan Mother?"

Anas'kala fidgeted, clearly nervous to be speaking to men. She looked up towards the sky, completely blotted out by the heavy foliage all around them. She took several moments to compose her reply, then spoke, looking into Datolo's eyes.

"When I saw the old man climbing up towards us, I was frightened. Then I saw he was some kind of healer or dreamer. We also have healers and dreamers, but mostly they are among the Mother men. I wondered how a man could do those things, when I saw the hunter and his sick child. I'm still wondering, but now I am no longer afraid."

"Yes. I understand that they are only unknown men, but..." Datolo paused, thinking before continuing, "we must know how many there are. We also need to see if they have Mother men among them. They may look weak, but they may not be much different from our clan. We need to know more, to know if they must be resisted, or killed, or if we will need to... find a new home. What say you Mokolo?"

Mokolo had listened, noticing how hard Datolo's last words were for him to speak. It was a fear he had kept inside, never telling anyone. The fear of losing the home of their ancestors. The fear of having to strike off in search of a peaceful, place that would support the lives of the clan. "I wanted to kill them when I first saw them. They took my father for no reason, I thought. Then I understood. It was their fear that forced their hands. When they came to the valley, it was to hunt game animals, not to kill us. Much the same as we hunt." He paused. Datolo nodded.

In a few moments, he added, "Now that I have seen the hunter trying to care for his sick child – a lesser mother child – then I felt something inside of his sadness and hurt. They may not be of our clan, but they are men who feel much as we do. If we learn more of them, maybe they can share this place with us. If there are not too many. But they fear us, and we need to be very careful."

Datolo then asked Baaktolo his thoughts. The maker drew his hand to his face, and looked down at the bed of spent cedar needles below them. "I also was afraid. Now, I see they are men, but I am still afraid because of how many there may be. I remember looking at their fires from high up near the falling of the river waters. There were so many fires it looked like fireflies in the distance. Their camp must be very large. We need to see it for ourselves and count their numbers before we can say if they be friend or enemy." He shook his head slowly, adding, "Until I know, they will remain enemies to me."

Datolo slapped his hand upon his chest, then raised both hands up vertically, signifying that everyone had spoken. He then asked Anask'ala, "Do you need to find help from the spirits to guide us, or can we proceed as hunters?"

"Should I accompany you farther?" She asked.

"Yes, I believe you need to see for the Clan Mother. Her eyes are with you. Did she tell you anything we need to know now?"

"You have already each spoken her words. They are just men, different, but also like us. We may need to fear them, or they may become friends, but we need to see more and count their numbers before we know. I will not seek the spirits, but I will find a quiet place nearby to ask the Great Mother for her help and to keep us in her protection while we are away from our home." She waited until Datolo had nodded, then she gathered her belongings to leave. Datolo asked her, "How long will you be gone?"

"As long as it takes. Wait for me."

"Will you be gone through the night? Should we return to see if the old man can cure the hunter's daughter?"

"No, I will return before the sun sets, and we will all return to see if the healing has been good."

Datolo nodded. He knew how to wait for a woman. Mother men had been telling him to wait his whole life.

Chapter 23

Anson felt a chill as the sun finally dipped below the far ridges. Gunda had not moved since she fell asleep. He didn't want her to be cold, and was about to speak when the Seer rose, unexpectedly, still singing, and disappeared into the rough, stone shelter crawling on hands and knees to enter. He quickly emerged, carrying another bearskin, still singing. Anson wondered how he could carry on so long and not have his voice break. The Seer stood over Gunda and covered her with the warm bearskin leaving her face exposed. He looked straight into Anson's eyes and nodded before returning to his position near the barely smoldering fire.

Anson was exhausted from his fear and worry and from sitting on bare stone for hours. He wondered how much longer this could continue. His answer came long after the moon had risen and again fallen, leaving them in almost complete darkness, just before the dawn. Stars and the few remaining embers of the Seer's fire were the only light in the world.

He had fallen asleep, despite his discomfort, in a sitting position, and had slumped over his folded legs. What woke him was the sun's first direct morning light striking his closed eyes. He stirred, then rolled to his left, almost striking his head on the stone. "Whaaa?" he muttered, then heard the Seer, still singing, but whose voice was now barely a croak.

Suddenly, the song ended. The Seer rose and with short, hopping steps, again danced around the stone circle three times, this time the other way around, finally stopping and kneeling next to Gunda. He lay his hands upon her head and she moaned in her sleep, then stirred and coughed a few times as she awoke. Anson waited for a signal from the Seer before jumping up and rushing to

Gunda's side. He asked her how she was feeling as the Seer brought her another water gourd.

When she wrinkled up her face, he said, "Drink child, it's only clear water." She did, greedily emptying the gourd. Anson asked her again as she finished, and she looked at him and replied, "I'm not as tired… but I'm kind of sore all over, and when I breathe, it still hur… hur.." she broke into a ragged cough dispelling any notion Anson had that she may have been cured. The Seer shook his head. He stood and turned his back on his small patient and her father as he raised his hands up towards the sky.

"I have listened all night and sung the song as I was told, yet you have not sent a spirit of healing to us! What must I do to save this child?" From the roughness and rage in his voice, Anson was sure the Seer had done everything he could. The realization crushed him. He sat, watching Gunda rub her eyes and wrap the bear skin tighter around her thin shoulders.

"I will bring us some food. You'll both need to eat. Some vision might come later, when I sleep, so don't worry. We're not finished… yet." The Seer touched Anson's shoulder as he spoke. What else could he do?

They were eating some dried meat, berries and acorn bread. No one spoke. Gunda would eat a few small bites, then cough a few times, then eat again. She was very weak, but still, Anson saw, had an appetite. It gave him a tiny bit of hope. He sat with his back to the forest, across the fire from the Seer and his daughter.

He saw Gunda's mouth fly open and her eyes suddenly go round with fear. She raised her arm and pointed over her father's shoulder. The Seer began to rise, reaching for his staff and Anson swung around to see a chilling sight. His breath caught in this throat and he began to reach for his bow and arrows.

The Seer stood, pulling himself up on his staff, but when Anson nocked an arrow, the Seer shook his head and lay his hand over the bowgrip, pulling it away from Anson.

"No! Wait! They have been sent to us... look!"

The brush was opening to allow three, no four trolls to slowly walk out, led by... led by what must be a child troll – a female, he guessed. The Seer pointed up to the sky, where Anson saw the large hawk had returned, this time from the direction of the forest, rising up and hovering over the rock surface as the three larger trolls stood shoulder to shoulder, while the child stepped out from them, holding a large deerskin bag in front of her.

Anson, terrified, but restrained by the Seer's frozen calm, asked "What do they want? Why are they here?"

"I saw the hawk and knew that they had been sent. I don't know why, but we must wait to see. The Seer returned to the spot where Anson had been sitting next to Gunda. She was now shaking and muttering to herself, with her head hidden beneath the bearskin. Anson leapt the fire and joined them, putting his arms around her but keeping his eyes on the trolls. They began making a chattering noise between themselves. It must be their speech, he thought. It didn't sound like any words he'd ever heard. It was low and made of clicks and grunts. They were just standing there. The three held spears with large, cruel points, but the child one... she simply held out her bag and looked all the time right at Gunda.

\#\#\#\#

Datolo still thought it was a bad idea to reveal themselves like this. He saw the hunter go for his weapons, and was about to throw his small spear when he also saw the old man take the Hunter's bent stick and small spears. He said to Anask'ala, 'You were right. They will hear us – or wait for us to show them what you have for the child."

"I knew I could help her." She replied. We used to have that illness among our children, too. The Clan Mother taught me to always bring the flowers for the cure when I travel anywhere, in case someone has need, and back in the forest, when I went to send my prayers, I found more. Many more of them."

Mokolo was so afraid he hoped he would not lose his water and bring them all shame. He didn't know that Baaktolo was thinking exactly the same thing. He wanted dry legs if he had to die, at least he would be strong for the clan and not a wet baby. As they stood there, looking at the two men and the sick child, Mokolo felt his fear begin to ebb. When the old man took the hunter's weapons, a heavy weight seemed to lift off his heart. Now, he felt the strength of his clan brother men and watched with admiration, the fearlessness of the Lesser Mother as she slowly reached into her burden and brought out two handfuls of beautiful, red flowers with some leaves attached. She lay down her bag, putting both of her now filled hands in front of her and began to slowly approach the three sitting on the rock. He hoped the Great Mother would protect her.

# # # #

"Look!" said the Seer, "she is bringing us something – flowers. Remain seated, no matter what she does, so she will not feel you are threatening her. She may be hideous to look at, but she has been sent with … maybe with a cure!"

"Do you really think a cure could come from horrid trolls? How could that be?" The approaching troll girl was almost as tall as he was, thickly built, with a huge mass of hair falling over a low, evil-looking forehead with black eyes set deep into her face, a broad, flat nose and a wide, gaping mouth. Her arms, reaching forward were almost covered with coarse, dark hair, but in her spread palms, she carried a large pile of beautiful red flowers he'd never seen before. She was getting closer and it was making him shiver with disgust and fear, but he held his place, for Gunda's sake. He held onto his shaking daughter.

"Anson, we never know everything that the Creator has to show us, only little bits here and there. Today, he is showing us something we need to know about trolls…" The Seer's speech was strained, almost spat out between his teeth. Anson heard the fear in the Seer's voice, if not in the words he was speaking. "Hold fast. The flowers may be a cure."

The troll girl was almost upon them, still holding out the flowers. She knelt down on the other side of the fire, and raised her palms up in a gesture of offering, then very gently, sat them down upon the bare stone. She motioned to the flowers, then to Gunda. She made the exact, same gesture again. Anson unwrapped the top of the bearskin to reveal his shaking daughter. As the troll girl child nodded and opened her wide mouth in… in a smile? Anson shivered at the sight, but thought it must be a smile.

Gunda opened her eyes and saw the troll girl through the fire and screamed sharply, trying to back away. Anson shook his head, *no*, and smoothed her hair, wiping her eyes. This time, she really took in the sight of a troll, kneeling there, right before her, with a pile of red flowers and a big, ugly grin on its… on her face. The troll was a she… a child, compared with the size of the three with spears remaining behind her by the forest. Gunda stopped shaking. *What was this going to be? Will we all die here?* She coughed several times and saw the troll girl child was not smiling, but was nodding as if she knew. The troll put her hands flat on her chest and coughed herself, then reaching down, she picked up a flower, and showed it to the three of them for a moment before she … ate it! Leaves and all! She then pointed to Gunda, nodding.

"She expects my daughter to eat those flowers?" What poison may they be?" Anson was gripping the Seer's arm so tightly that his nails broke the skin, and a small trickle of blood coursed down the Seer's lanky old arm.

"She does, indeed. You can let go before you break it." He shook his arm loose, and Anson, to his horror, saw he'd hurt the old man.

I'm so sorry. I'm…"

"Look – she is trying to tell us something." The Seer held the small wounds on his arm while the troll girl child spoke for a time in her chattering gibberish. He shook his head to show her he did not understand, so she raised one hand, palm out, and then, pointing to Gunda, counted by pressing a finger into the palm, four times.

"Four! Gunda should eat four flowers. But when? How often?" His eyes darted back and forth and Anson saw fear there. Finally, he simply bent both elbows, and put his palms up.

The troll girl child seemed to understand. She again counted out four fingers upon an open palm, then moved her hand in an arc above herself. She did it again, first pointing to where the sun rose, and finally pointing where the sun fell behind the ridges. She was about to repeat it when the Seer suddenly shouted out "Four! Every day!" He was nodding, then his eyes clouded again as he asked out loud, … "All at once? Should she eat them, all at once?" He pointed to Gunda and put out his palms then swung his own hand over head.

The troll girl child seemed puzzled. She looked down at the flowers, then quickly picked up her head, smiling again as she again counted, but this time she counted … one… two then stopped and made the arc, only going up a little bit from the sunrise place, then counted out one…two and made the arc, stopping just before the sunset place. She stared into the Seer's face and repeated the whole process again. This time, when she was halfway through, he understood, shouting and smiling, "Two flowers in the morning and two more in the evening! Four flowers in all each day! Anson are you seeing this?"

Anson, now almost speechless, watching a troll girl, child ... healer, explain the details of the treatment his daughter needed. Language didn't work, but she and the Seer understood each other. They must have been sent by the Creator! "I can barely believe this is happening... I don't know how... I don't know..." his voice trailed off and a look of almost goofy happiness began to brighten his face. The Seer's face was by now covered by a huge grin. Tears were streaming down his cheeks. He nodded over and over to the troll girl child and watched as she stood and returned to her bundle, returning with it. She dumped out two more hands full of the flowers, and then counted out enough for many days. The Seer kept track. Sixteen days in all. She carefully gathered the rest into her bag and stood, raising one arm up, palm out facing the two men and the small sick girl. She then said some more of her clicking noises and looked up at the sky.

Anson and the Seer both stood, and also raised their hands up, then also looked at the sky, where they saw the large hawk had returned from across the lake and was circling above them. It cried out sharply three times, then flew off to the forest. As it did, the troll girl child returned to her comrades, who also raised one hand, palm out. In a blink, they had disappeared back into the brush as silently as they had made their approach. On the flat stone surface, two men and a small girl remained behind, rubbing their eyes in disbelief. Had this really happened? But there, on the stone right beside their feet, lay a pile of red flowers neither man had ever seen before.

The Seer picked up two of them. "Gunda, you will have to eat two of these each morning and two each evening until you are well. I'd like you to try them now."

Gunda shook her head, crying "But... they came from
a ... from a troll! I can't eat them!"

Anson took them from the Seer's outstretched hand
and hugged his daughter. He held her face in both hands
and said, "Yes you will, daughter. These were sent to us
as medicine for your cure, by the Spirit that created us all!
The trolls were only used to carry them to us." He handed
one to Gunda, who sniffed her tears away and slowly put
it in her mouth. As she chewed it, she said "It's sweet and
bitter, too... it kind of tingles my tongue!" she smiled and
reached for the second flower. Then she asked her father,
"Did you see the troll girl? She ate one, too!"

"Yes, Of course, I did. I saw her eat one, too." He
hugged her so tightly he thought he might break her, but
she only hugged back with as much strength as she could
muster. He began to think it was going to be alright.
Everything was going to be alright. Maybe even the fear
of the trolls would change now. They were ugly, but
maybe they weren't so bad after all. They didn't look like
stone, just like ugly men.

As he gathered up his pack frame and the rest of their
belongings, he wanted to ask so many questions of the
Seer, and offer him the very next deer he killed, but the
Seer simply put up his hand. When he spoke, it was with
great solemnity.

"Nothing of this, Anson, will return to the village
with you. You will not speak of the trolls at all. They were
simply the means of carrying the flowers and we still
don't know if they will help Gunda. We will wait. I have
a great deal to think about, so I will not accompany you
back, I will remain to ask my own questions and find
answers in my dreams. Do you agree? NO speaking of
this?"

Anson's mood changed instantly. He didn't
understand why the news wouldn't be shared with

everyone. "I don't understand… this is a good thing, isn't it?"

"I'm not sure yet. You must trust me with this knowledge alone. If you need to speak with anyone, speak with me and no one else. Not even Gudrun or your other children. You may tell them that the flowers were from me. If I determine that it is safe to share this then I will tell you and you may, but NOT UNTIL I TELL YOU. Do you agree?" The Seer thrust out his hand and arm to Anson.

"Of course, I trust you on this matter. I will keep this between us until I hear from you otherwise." He clasped the Seer's arm. He then asked, "What about Gunda?"

The Seer approached the girl, saying quietly but sternly, "Gunda, you must eat the flowers every day at morning and evening, as I have told you. If anyone asks you where they came from, you will tell them I gave them to you, but you will not tell anything else that happened here. It might bring danger to the village if you do. Do you agree, girl?"

Gunda nodded, sniffing. She put out her small thin arm, and said, "Yes, Seer, nothing of what we saw or did here will be told to anyone. It will be a secret for just us." She tried to clasp his arm, but her fingers didn't go all the way around. All three chuckled, which set Gunda off on a coughing jag.

Chapter 24

Anson and his daughter walked together, to the Seer's house. It was a sunny day and time for more of the red flowers. She walked carefully beside her father, not as sure on her feet as she once had been, but still, she was walking. *The flowers*, thought Anson, his hand guiding her as she moved, *the troll's flowers have saved her.* She hadn't coughed but two or three times that day and the bitter water the Seer had prepared helped her sleep each night. It had been seven nights so far, but the past three days she had improved steadily and was even eating like her old self. No one knew where the flowers had come from, only that the Seer had given them to Gunda. Not even her mother knew the truth, a fact that troubled Anson. He had never held anything back from Gudrun, and this was new territory. He hoped it would not be long before the Seer told him they could share the truth.

Up ahead, he saw Nils sitting outside the Seer's doorway. The Seer's house was set apart from the rest of the village, nearer to the council fire pit and its door was turned to face the lake. Gunda was not paying attention to where she was going and she ran into her father, almost tripping.

"Look! Fish!" she cried, her voice expressing excitement for the first time in many, many days.

Anson saw the spreading rings on the lake surface and replied, "You are right Gunda. Should we go fishing?"

"Yes. As soon as we get more flowers, let's all go fishing together!" Her little face was beaming. Anson thought of the troll girl, kneeling before the fire with her red flowers. He silently thanked the Creator and the sprits for their help. He had been thanking them almost constantly for days now.

"Anson!" Nils called out to him, his hand raised in greeting.

They approached and Anson replied, "Nils! It's good to see you. Nils, this is my youngest daughter, Gunda..." he motioned to his right, where she had been walking, but found her hiding behind his legs.

"It's good to see you, but better to see her looking so well." Nils said, smiling. He stood and walked down from where he'd been sitting, to join them. "Come, child, let me see you." He said to Gunda.

Anson gently guided her around his legs to meet the village leader, who knelt down to speak with her.

Gunda smiled at Nils, saying, "Hello... my name is Gunda."

Nils laughed out loud, replying, "Yes! Yes it is! How are you feeling today, Gunda?"

"Oh. I feel nice today. I saw a big fish!" she replied, adding, "We're all going fishing!"

Nils patted her head, then stood up, saying, "That sounds like a good idea! Let's not keep the Seer waiting any longer." In a few steps, they were all three entering the dark doorway of the Seer, whose voice could be heard croaking from the shadows, in a chanted song. Anson recognized it as a song of thanks. They sat on the log in the center of the room, and the Seer joined them, with a small smoking lamp. It added scarcely any light to the dark room, but it sent dancing shadows into motion along the walls where all manner of dried plants and bones and... other things were tied. Gunda wrinkled up her nose at the disagreeable smell and the smoke of the lamp, but she knew to remain silent.

The Seer rose, and retrieved a basket full of the withered red flowers. He sat down and counted out enough for the next seven days, then dropped them into the deerskin bag that Anson had brought along with them.

"This will speed her healing for another seven days." He told Anson. "She is feeling stronger?"

"Yes, Seer, and she is sleeping through the night with the bitter water." The Seer nodded and the asked Gunda to stand. She did, slowly, leaning upon her father's shoulders. He watched, then asked her to turn all the way around three times. She did so, only faltering once as she passed her father's shoulder. Finally she stood still, and leaned against Anson as she waited.

"Gunda, how do you feel right now?" the Seer asked her.

I feel a little dizzy, but alright, except… we're going fishing!"

"That is what I had hoped you'd tell me." He winked at her which made her giggle, then she coughed once.

"You must eat the red flowers for a few more days. Is that good?"

"It's … it's alright. They taste funny, but they don't taste bad or anything."

She leaned on Anson a bit more and the Seer noticed, saying, "Gunda it is fine for you to sit back down." Anson smiled at the Seer's consideration. He waited, wondering why Nils was with them.

# # # #

Mokolo stretched his stiff legs and arms once he'd joined the rest on the ground. It had been many nights sleeping in trees, and now he was so sore and tired, even a rock would be more comfortable. His legs were so stiff he could barely stand. Still, it felt good to know that when they returned they would bring news that they could share with the clan. It had been worth it; even the risk that Anas'kala had taken had been worth it. Her courage filled the three men with pride.

Datolo motioned them all to gather near him. He bade them sit around him, and he passed out the remaining dried meat. Yesterday, they had covered the last part of their journey home quickly, but still had to sleep in a tree with no fire. Even though they were close, he wanted to take no further chances of being followed. He spoke quietly to them while they chewed. "You have all done your very best and tolerated poor sleeping, hard travel and bad food for many days. Today we return to our home. You should all be proud of the task we've accomplished. We have a great deal to share with the Clan Mother and with the rest." He clapped his hand against his chest, acknowledging the accomplishment. They all responded likewise, then he asked, "Helper of the Clan Mother, what say you?"

Anas'kala replied "I say thank you to the Great Mother for keeping us safe, and for holding the other men's weapons still." She collected her far-ranging thoughts, and recalled the regular expanse of odd, box-like dwellings with pointed tops stretching off away from the end of the lake and the many women and children she saw washing and playing in the water. Before her mind reeled, she brought herself back to the small group and continued, "Our Great Mother knows the other men and their ways seem strange to us, but she stilled our fear and led me to show them that we could help them. I am glad. You three were strong and you guided us through danger. I say thank you for that as well." She clapped her chest, then added, "and I will be very glad to sleep in my own bed tonight, with my own sisters around me!"

The three men looked at each other, then in unison, clapped their own chests and began to laugh. Anas'kala had never laughed openly with men before. But there had been so much unspoken tension that before she gave it a second thought, the laughter just flew out of her.

####

The Seer had been speaking in an oddly loud voice for some time now as Anson realized he hadn't really been listening. He had stopped listening when the Seer began describing how his vision led him to a strange grove of trees he'd never noticed before, and how below them, on the ground, were clusters of beautiful, deep red flowers, growing in circles…

"…and there, I was struck by another vision from the Creator showing me gathering them then Gunda eating them and being healed. In my vision, she glowed like the sun! Now it has come to pass and she will be cured of her ills."

Nils began listening intently to every word the Seer spoke. All of it was lies except Gunda being saved by the red flowers. When the Seer stopped, Nils raised his chin up from his hands where it had rested through the entire story. He said only, "I see." He looked at Anson, then at Gunda. Anson knew he was expecting their words in assertion of the Seer's tale.

Anson quickly squeezed his daughter's hand as he spoke, saying "Yes, it was a miracle! The flowers have cured her, or will, when she has finished them." He gave her hand another squeeze hoping she would understand.

"Now can we go fishing?" She couldn't have chosen better words. Nils immediately broke into laughter and the Seer joined him, still a bit loudly to Anson's ears. Anson felt he must also laugh and he picked up his daughter and sat her on his lap while she clapped her hands at the joke. It seemed to be an effective ruse, and Nils rose, thanked the Seer for his wisdom and help and left.

The Seer stopped laughing as soon as Nils left the house. He appeared puzzled when he looked at Anson, but said only. "There. You both did well. We will keep this secret for the time being."

He rose and showed them out, then returned to his darkness as Anson and Gunda were left standing in the late afternoon sun, blinking as their eyes settled back into the light of day. He slowly led his daughter by the hand, down, around the council fire pit and gathering space, then out along the planks laid in the lake shore to the water's edge.

"I'd like to walk in the water, can I do that?"

Anson thought about it, then replied, "Yes, but take off your shoes first, and don't stay in too long. I'll watch you from the bank over there. Will you come when I call you?"

"Yes. I'll come back when you call me and I won't go out very far. I just want to see some more fish jump."

He found a spot to sit down and lean back into the sloping bank and watched as Gunda pulled off her deerskin shoes and began to splash and stomp around in the soft, squishy mud she loved. The sunlight sparkled on the water in countless places, like tiny fires, dancing all the way across the lake until they blended together. His daughter's yellow hair seemed ablaze, too. He tried to savor the joy in the sight, but deep inside, the uncertainty of what he had just been part of, gnawed at him. He waited a few more moments, until he saw she was tiring slightly, and called her out of the lake and back to him. As he did, Nils approached.

"Anson! Can you speak with me for a moment?"

"Of course!" He grasped the man's arm and helped him down to recline along the bank as Gunda slid her shoes back on, still down by the lake.

After speaking for a few moments, Nils stood and took his leave, just as Gunda returned, sitting down next to her father. "Are we still going fishing? I saw some more big ones jump."

Anson put his arm around her and noticed she was shivering slightly. "No, I'm sorry, but the day is leaving and it will be too cold to fish today. We will fish tomorrow, though I promise you."

Gunda bit her lip and looked petulant, but kept still. He added, "I'm sure your mother has a wonderful meal ready for us. Are you hungry yet?"

"Yes, I'm hungry right now!" She jumped to her feet and tugged on her father's hand to pull him up. He was glad to see her disappointment had faded. Tomorrow would be soon enough. They walked home, talking about fish, and hawks, and while Anson still had a vague worry working away in his heart, he let it slip away while they walked back home. He looked down and said, "Gunda – you kept your shoes clean – no mud. You mother will be proud of you."

Gunda gave him a smile that he thought was even brighter than the sun on the lake. Still, Anson felt darkness pressing him. Nils had simply confirmed the Seer's story again. The Seer had not told Nils the truth of how Gunda had been cured, and now Nils wanted to plan another hunting party into the trolls' valley. *This time*, he'd said, *we'll find out where they hide. Then we can get rid of them all.* Anson struggled with that. Besides saving Gunda's life, the trolls did not attack them even though they could have. Anson was also beginning to also think of the high valley as belonging to the trolls, not as a seasonal extension of the traditional hunting range for the village.

But he kept these thoughts to himself. As he and his daughter walked along the pathways between their neighbor's homes, he decided he'd have to speak with the Seer again. Before the next hunt. He'd planned it for the morning after the next great moon, six suns away. He counted the last of the red flowers. Enough to last morning and evening, five more full days. He would bring Gunda, to speak with the Seer as well, just to make sure she was cured.

Chapter 25

"There are reasons. Important reasons... why we cannot tell of the trolls'... help. It...." The Seer's voice trailed off as he gazed up into the darkness of his foul-smelling hovel. Gunda was sitting near the door, which Anson had left open so she could watch the lake. He knew to wait. Give the Seer time to answer.

"There have been... prophecies. Do you understand that? Seers back in line to my father's, father's, father received visions of the last of the trolls, from the Creator - - of what must pass. Of what must happen." The Seer's eyes were bright, and he looked into Anson's face with such purpose Anson felt afraid. He swallowed, then replied, "Yes, I know what that means, but I have never heard of these."

"It is just as well, as they are to be secret. Only Nils knows of them, but you have been a part in what must follow, so I can tell you. Will you hear?"

"Yes, Seer, I will hear the visions... the prophecies of what must pass."

"The Seer of old, dreamt a dream of a village. Happy, safe, set high above a lake where no enemies could reach it. He saw as the enemies faded away. First the big lions, then the bears, but still, one enemy hid in the shadows. The trolls hid themselves, far up, among the rocks above a valley full of game, with a small river, full of fish. Eagles flew on the breezes, high above, sending down the blessings of the Creator."

Anson though for a moment, then said, "Yes, that is the same as the stories. They tell of villages rising where enemies have departed. But why must we not speak of the trolls help? Maybe they are not enemies after all, but just other men?"

"No. They are not other men. You should know better. Did you not see them? See how ugly they were? Did you not smell them?"

"Yes, of course… but there are those among us who are not beautiful. It makes them no less than the rest."

The Seer drew back from Anson, then touched his arm, saying, "There are prophecies that speak of defeating the trolls… what must be done for a village to find peace and safety, for our children's safety. If these things are not done, then the prophecies will be broken, and we will all suffer." He gazed up to the darkness above, then added, "Don't you see? Either we have power, or the trolls have power. One must prevail, one must die or be driven away… we can't share with the likes of trolls and even another village of men would threaten our safety and peace. Do you remember the thieves that stole our women and children? They might have been other men, but they were enemies, too."

Anson nodded. Part of what the Seer had said was true. Their village now sat near the lake because another village had been built near to where they used to live. Soon, the game was gone and the raiding had begun. They had all come here for peace and safety. "I know that what you say has been true, but… the trolls helped us. They didn't hurt us. Why must they be driven from their own home?"

The Seer laid his ancient, gnarled hand upon Anson's shoulder, replying," They must be driven away because of the prophecies. Have my visions ever failed us? Have I ever led us astray or into danger?"

The Seer's eyes were again burning into his mind. He considered the question. The answer was not clear, as it had been The Seer that led them to the lake in the first place. If the trolls were enemies, then he had led them into danger. He didn't understand how to answer. If the trolls wanted friendship, how was that a stroke against The

Seer. He felt there must be something that the Seer feared from them, even if they became friends to the village.

In the end, he simply shook his head: no. He had no more questions besides the ones remaining in his heart that he would have to answer for himself, but he knew, for certain, that he would have to tell his wife what had happened up the mountain and tell her where the red flowers had come from. He also knew that the Seer would never tell anyone what had happened. What did the Seer really fear? He turned to where his daughter had been sitting near the door, but Gunda was nowhere to be seen. He turned back to the Seer, saying,

"Thank you for speaking with me. I must find my daughter. She has wandered away outside."

The Seer rose smiling, clapping his hand against his chest. The session was over. He had prevailed and Anson would keep the secret. Anson hurried outside to find Gunda.

Anson saw her only a few strides away, quietly stacking rocks she'd found nearby. "See my mountains?" she called to Anson as he joined her.

"Yes, they are tall."

"Now watch me," she said in a serious tone, as she locked her hands together and flapped them like a bird's wings. "See? I'm a hawk! See the hawk's shadow?"

Her flapping hands set a shadow over the stacks of rocks that resembled the way the hawk's shadow passed over them that day as they sat upon the Seer's flat overhanging rock. Anson scooped her right up, hoping, as he carried her home, she would not soon be making little twig trolls with red flowers.

# # # #

The fire had died to red embers as he and Gudrun knelt upon the floor near her hearth. Anson was speaking in low, hushed tones, so the children would not wake. Gudrun's eyes grew bigger and rounder with each thing he told her.

"Across the fire, through the smoke, we watched as they stepped silently from the woods where they had been hiding. Three big trolls with nasty black spears and one more... a young... girl troll, too...."

Gudrun's hand flew to her mouth to stifle a moan. "Anson!" she whispered.

"Yes. I'm telling you the truth."

"Were you afraid?"

"Of course! I was terrified, and angry, and confused. Why had the Seer not protected us, I thought." Anson continued the story, as his wife reacted to each mention of the trolls or the troll girl child, shaking with fear. As he neared the end, Gudrun relaxed a bit, then began to nod her head as he made each point. "She made signs to tell us how many flowers Gunda should eat, and when. She... she must be one of their healers. She knew things the Seer didn't know. She..." His voice broke as he finished his story, "...she saved our daughter, and then they melted away into the woods as if they had never been there at all."

Gudrun shuddered, then touched Anson's arm. "How can I believe you? This is ... this is just too hard to believe. Are you sure it wasn't a vision while you slept?"

He shook his head. "No, every word is true. We owe Gunda's life to the trolls who helped us. Nothing the Seer did, helped her." He looked into Gudrun's eyes. She wasn't yet convinced, so he added, "Find a quiet time tomorrow, and ask Gunda what happened the day we climbed the mountain. Press her for details, and tell her that I said it was alright for her to share our secret with you, but only with you. She will tell you what she saw, with her own eyes."

Gudrun nodded, silently. She knew children did not tell false stories. She would ask Gunda to tell her story, but for now, she wanted to know what Anson was going to do.

"I... I can't do anything. I can't tell anyone, because they won't believe me, and it would go against the Seer's words. He won't tell the truth, and I can't understand why. If the trolls want to be friends, and not kill us or steal our children, why not share the news with everyone? It is madness not to, but I fear the Seer's wrath."

Gudrun replied, "The Seer must know things... secret things. That must be why he didn't tell the truth."

"I don't believe it. I heard his... reasons... and they were just the same as the old stories told again. He didn't know any more than you or I know about trolls. He has another reason, but I can't figure it out in time to stop this next hunting trip into the upper valley." He stopped and took both her arms in his hands, adding, "I don't want to repay the kindness that troll girl child showed us by ... by killing them. By killing some of us as well." Anson's eyes glistened as tears formed. His hands shook. "There is nothing I can do."

Gudrun lay her hands on his. She crossed her arms upon her breast, asking, "You won't tell Nils?"

"How can I? He doesn't do anything without consulting the Seer, first. Why would he believe my words, anyway? I feel that if I could only understand the Seer's fear, then I would know what to do..." He hung his head down until his chin rested on his chest. Gudrun touched his cheek to soothe him. It was a serious problem. She turned it around and around in her mind. They sat silently huddled together for a time, then it came to her. She spoke quietly.

"Anson, could the reason the Seer wants to keep this secret is because... because the troll girl child is a better healer? She has more power than he does, and he wants to protect his position in the village? Is it possible that's the reason?" She went on, "Suppose he told the truth, and everyone learned that the old stories about trolls may not be true? Then we would not fear them, and we might learn things from them that he does not know. Better medicine, maybe even better ways of seeking visions or speaking with the spirits… what then?" Anson looked up, but did not reply. Gudrun added, "Would anyone even listen to anything he said, now knowing he had kept the truth from us all?"

"No. No one would listen to him. He would have to find work he could do to stay with us. He would have to kill his own meat, gather his own food. As long as everyone believes his words, he won't have to." Anson jumped to his feet, suddenly, saying out loud, "That's why he wants us to keep quiet!"

"SHHH! You'll wake the village!" Gudrun pulled him back down to join her once more. "That is why you will keep the secret. He knows ways… ways to hurt, ways to kill without being seen. We are not safe now, and it will be worse for us all if you tell anyone else. Do you agree?"

"Yes, I understand, but still… something must be done. If our chief will not make peace with them, at least the trolls must be… warned. How can I do that? I'm supposed to lead the hunt for them myself!" He looked deeply into his wife's face for a sign that she might have an idea. After a moment, it seemed that she did.

Chapter 26

The team's new excavation at the site in Norway was almost complete. The in-situ remains of four adult humans of what appeared to be the Neanderthaler species lay revealed as the last of the compacted clay was brushed off. The entire thing had become very puzzling. Dr. Ariel Conner and her site foreman Jens stood quietly watching the last bucket of clay dust and fragments lifted to the team member who would sift it for every possible clue.

"This doesn't make any sense…" Jens mused.

"You've already said that. It's not shedding any light on what we have here, Jens. Why don't we work from this burial site backwards, to our original notes. Let's assume that this is exactly what it looks like."

"Ariel, it's too far North for Neanderthalers." His words almost conveyed anger. This was so far outside of their soon-to-be-published findings, he couldn't settle his thoughts.

"Yes. Of course, you're right, but… here they are. Would you agree that these are not modern humans?"

"Yes. Clearly they are not. The oversized craniums and low brow ridges confirm that. All the skeletal remains suggest a typical Neanderthaler burial site. The interment of what appear to be spears and the basket of beads and stone implements have been seen before, but down near the Mediterranean. The Spanish burial site comes to mind."

Ariel scratched her eyebrow as a small fly buzzed away. The rock cleft they stood in lay close above the habitation cave. It was narrow at the bottom, barely four meters wide. The air was musty and the heat and humidity were making it very unpleasant. She tried to mentally gather all the signs that would have made this an unlikely site for burial relics and skeletal remains to have been preserved, yet there was the evidence, below her feet.

She could barely stifle her desire to blurt out the obvious, that this was, indeed a Neanderthaler burial and habitation site, despite the late Stone Age tools and artifacts. Especially the large fertility figure. Female forms such as the one they had recovered here had only been discovered in the habitation and ceremonial sites of modern humans, often with paintings and animal track graphics. Certainly not the earlier Neanderthaler. They had proposed, in their paper's final conclusion that this site had been a modern human habitation dating to around 35000 BCT, but it seemed now, they were wrong. It was either an earlier site, showing a much, much farther Northern extent of the range of the Neanderthalers than had previously been considered, or it was… some kind of proof that the two species had occupied a range together.

"Ariel? Any thoughts?"

"Sorry, Jens, I was lost for a moment there. Let's recap: we have major conflicts not just here at this burial site, but also in the habitation cave sites. The tools near the excavated hearths are much finer than typical for Neanderthaler sites, the fertility paintings and the figure in the rear cleft inside the cave are not right either… but here, we have another conflict, as they don't really correspond to fertility figures and symbols for Late Stone Age Modern Human sites in the record. Finally we have the wrong type of burial and the wrong type of skeletal remains… I think we have to rethink our entire thesis regarding this site."

Jens nodded, his hand to his chin. Months and months of work.

"Dr. Conner? Can you see these?" One of the excavation crew, a student, was shining a strong flashlight beam into the exposed ribcage of one of the skeletons. Something twinkled as the light struck it.

"Yes, there's something there. Can you retrieve it? Get a photo first. Take two or three."

"Okay." The dig worker called for the photographer. "Haakon? Can you get some shots here?"

After some scrambling around, and maybe six shots including some close-ups, the student held up their gloved hand, palm up, and approached the edge of the excavation. Ariel stooped down, and lifted the small, fluted stone arrowhead from her student's palm. "How many other men are down there?"

"The student, bent down, then replied, "I see four right now, besides the one in your hand. They all appear to be of the same stone. It reminds me of the Lake site. Remember the chert outcropping and all the axes and knives?"

"Yes. I see the similarity." Ariel held the arrowhead up between her thumb and forefinger, and turned her hand to catch the light. This was almost certainly the same work and the same stone as their last excavation, in the valley, down below along the shore of an ancient lake. The water had been long gone, but the excavation found many stone tools and the traces of wooden posts of a large Late-Stone age/ Early Bronze Age community. She held the arrowhead up to Jens Erickksen, who took it and after it over a few times, nodded his head in excitement.

"This is almost exactly the same point as those we gathered from the Lake site! We found nothing made of this rock here at all. What is this?"

The student in the excavation called up to them, "Oh! We have one more point. This one's embedded in one of the cervical vertebra, in the back, I can just... I can just clear the clay away... here." They called over the camera again, and the photographer had to kneel right down in the grave to get the shot after a hole beside the skeleton's neck was enlarged to hold the camera.

"Jens, any ideas now?"

He smiled, and replied, "Looks like a murder victim to me. Adult male, Neanderthaler, killed by probably an arrow… or six."

"Right, Jens, but who shot the arrows? Why did they kill him?"

Jens was already thinking of how much more work would be needed now. This excavation might be the one that would make his career. He wondered if he could re-craft the whole thing in the form of a murder mystery, maybe…

"We're going to have to extend this excavation, back to the rock face where it ends. There may be additional graves." She then explained to her mapping assistant who had joined them along the edge of the pit, "You should also take a team and climb the face, then walk back along whatever lies up above, just in case there are more burials up there… anything, really."

Chapter 27

"We'll keep the secret, for now. Just the three of us will know." Gudrun spoke to her husband and her youngest daughter. She'd been out gathering some berries with Gunda when she asked the little girl of the things that had happened at the top of the ridge, with the Seer. Gunda was happy to tell her story. It confirmed everything Anson had said, but knowing it was true did not make her feel relieved. It made her more uneasy. Anson was right, something had to be done. She mulled over how she would explain her idea to their other children.

Anson didn't like it at first. It meant he'd have to bring Gunda with him, which he was dead set against, but then, Gudrun suggested that she also come along. This terrified him. "It's bad enough to risk our daughter's safety and health, but to risk my wife, too? How could I allow that? Have you forgotten the bears… how about the knife tooth lions?"

"You would be risking your own safety if you went alone, would you not? Even with an entire hunting party, there are risks. Raaka knew them."

"But why? Why would you need to come, or Gunda, for that matter?"

The discussion had revolved around this for some moments now, and Gudrun had to find a way to help him understand. She looked up and followed the smoke rising from their roof. Far above, she saw a shadow pass through the smoke. A hawk was circling far above them. It brought the story back to her.

"When you sat with the Seer, at his fire, four trolls crept up to you, but they didn't attack you, or hurt any of you in any way. They could have, but didn't. Why do you suppose?"

"I… I don't know for sure. It made me even more afraid, at first, wondering what they were going to do."

"I'm a mother. I know why. Gunda. They saw your daughter and stopped. She will protect you, at least from trolls, but you will need to protect her from all the other dangers. I can help you do that."

"But what of the children? Surely we can't all... just disappear?"

"No. But if they remained behind and also knew how Gunda was cured, it would not remain a secret long. We will have to disappear, the three of us." Gudrun's eyes started to tear, but she wiped them and continued, adding, "Haakon and Hege can take care of the house until we return. We'll tell them... that Gunda needs more flowers. If they need to explain our absence to anyone else, it will make sense and after we return it won't matter. I'll tell them that Gunda is afraid of the Seeker and that we won't be away long. They can eat meals with my sister's family if they get lonely. How long do you think we will need?"

Anson was amazed at his wife's quick grasp of the situation and fearless planning. He began to count days, setting as a destination point in his mind, the spot where they encountered the trolls when they had been hunting and... probably killed one or more of them. He felt a distinct chill as he recalled the moment in the tall grass by the little river. He added four more days for further travel in the high valley, and two days for travel to the falls where the high valley began and the return. "Eight days should be enough, if we travel fast and meet no... enemies. We will have to travel unseen after we pass the outpost. We'll follow the game trails in the trees... gathering flowers. If we follow the small river, we will be far enough away from the bears on one side and the lions on the other..."

He paused and looked deeply into Gudrun's eyes, asking, "Are you sure? I can go with Gunda and you can stay here and ... explain my absence."

"No... I... I want to help you protect Gunda,' she replied, her eyes downcast.

"But if I travel as fast as I know I can with Gunda on my back, we will be protected. I know the closest part of that valley. I know where we can shelter along the river banks." He believed he must convince his wife to stay. Only she would look after Hege and Haakon as a mother would... if he and Gunda were lost.

"But, have you really thought about what you'll do when you find them... the trolls? You have said you can't understand their gibberish. How will this work? How can you make explanation? Can you keep Gunda safe?"

# # # #

Nils waited for his response. They sat together in the chief's house, along with the younger hunter Kells and two more. Nils had called them together to plan the hunt for the trolls. He spoke to them relaying the things the Seer had told him that would protect them. Nils wanted them to leave before the next moon, but Anson disagreed, finally adding, "It is too soon following my sighting of them on the falls. They may still be active around the entrance to the Valley. We need to wait another moon. Is there any new sighting? Has anyone been hurt or... any child stolen?"

Nils nodded. "No, you are right. There have been no more trolls seen since you saw them, or think you saw them last, and none have approached the outpost." He scratched his chin, then asked, "What say the rest of you?"

The other hunters, none of them anxious to begin this dangerous hunt, voiced their approval of waiting at least another moon or even two more. Kells added, "We'll have two more moons at least before all the leaves are down, and maybe when the trees are almost bare, we'll be able see further into the woods as we pass. It might be safer."

Nils absorbed this. It made some sense. He stood as did the rest, and it was agreed that the hunt for the trolls would be put off two more moons, until the most favorable time the Seer could determine from his dreams. They clapped their chests in unison and left the chief's house. As Anson was stepping through the door, Nils touched his arm and asked about Gunda's health.

"Gunda? She's feeling much better now. She is only coughing a little at night. I think she is almost cured – getting stronger every day." Anson's heart sank at his deception. Gunda was as well as she'd ever been. No thanks to the Seer.

"Good. You'll be sure to thank the Seer when you can?"

"Yes. Thank the Seer for all his help." Anson smiled and quickly left. He had one day before he had to spend three at the outpost, then, when he returned… there was just enough time. He wondered how he'd manage it all.

Chapter 28

"It was a terrible risk, but it was the right decision. I'm proud of you." The Clan Mother embraced her daughter's daughter in the near darkness. Anas'kala returned her embrace, despite the Mother's terrible odor. The ancient woman had not smelled the same for a long time now, and it worried the girl. She stepped back as soon as she could without angering the Mother.

Gathering the baskets, now empty of the herbs she had brought, she asked her grandmother, "Mother? Are you well? You seem far away."

"I am still with you. Don't fear for me." She patted Anas'kala on her arm, then spoke again, saying "Anas'kala, do you remember the stories of how our clan came to this valley?"

"Yes, Mother, I remember them."

"Then, you will remember that the Clan Mother at that time, received visions from the Great Mother that led us here. But, do you know why the clan left its home?"

Anas'kala shook her head.

"It was because new men came to the clan's home and tried to kill them all. Even the children."

Anas'kala shuddered and her eyes began to tear. The Clan Mother comforted her, saying, "Hush, hush my dear. Don't cry over things long past. Those were hard times, when the ice rose above all the valleys and there was little to eat. All of our clans journeyed towards the mid-day sun, to escape the cold. Our clan was among the last to find new homes, when the situation got especially dire. The other men made war with us, chasing us away so that they might save their own families...." She began to sob, herself, remembering secret stories only she knew of that time, so long ago.

"You cry Mother? Have I done something to offend you?"

"No, my darling, no. I just never expected that we would ever have to leave our valley or fight with the other men. They came later then we, but they were cruel and did not understand us or our ways. It was better to flee then, and if they come here, it will again be the only thing we can do... you can do."

"I can do? What do you mean Mother?" Anas'kala's hear grew heavy and worry clouded her eyes.

"You, my daughter's daughter... will lead our clan when I am gone. I have decided. I feel my time rapidly escaping me. Not yet, but not far to come. Do you understand me?"

"Me?" Anas'kala's voice shook, adding, "But I'm not worthy of such a great honor. I have only shown my moon blood one time and I have no children!"

"Still, when I heard what you had done... to help the young girl from the other men... then I knew. You will be the right one to bring our clan to safety, in the direction of the mid-day sun. To a new home, where you can live with no fear. I may yet make the journey with you."

Anas'kala's hand flew to her lips, as if to stop herself from speaking. She stood mute as the Clan Mother continued her explanation and instruction.

"Our people have been driven from their homes countless times now, since the coming of the Other men. We never understood why they seemed to hate us so. They had their own places, their own hunting land – there was really room for everyone, yet still they attacked us and we attacked them. Stories were handed down, mother to mother. The Great Mother sent us visions to follow the path of the mid-day sun to find new homes, and we have always followed her. Clan after clan, down through ages until so few of us remain..." Her eyes grew distant, and she swallowed several times. Anas'kala leaned over to offer her hand.

"No, child, I am fine… I just grow sad. I see soon it will be our time to travel our way towards the sun path and find a new home." Tears began to run down her leathery cheeks, and Anas'kala offered her a scrap of deerskin to wipe them. "Soon, Anas'kala, your true training will begin. Can you accept what the Great Mother has prepared for you?"

"Y…yes, Mother, I can. I will lead our clan as you have. I only hope I will find a way to grow in wisdom."

The Clan Mother smiled her toothless, red smile, wiping away the last of the tears. "It came to me to learn and grow, much as it has come to you. I learned. If you carry love for your clan in your heart always, it is the place where the Great Mother dwells inside you. She will share her wisdom, if you only listen to her." Anas'kala nodded, slowly and the Clan Mother added, "Don't worry. Everything will eventually be fine. Hardships always lead to comfort, as death leads to new life." She reached up her hand and laid it upon Anas'kala's chest.

"Thank you, Mother… but I'm sorry, too."

"What are you sorry for, daughter?"

"I'm sorry I helped the other men. It would have been better if we had remained hidden."

"No need to feel you made a mistake, daughter. You protected their girl's life. That is always your task. Even if the life is from… from the Other men. You did not make our trouble. It was always coming to us. Age after age, we leave when they arrive. Now, at least we know that our time is short here, so we can fully prepare to follow the sun to a new home. Dry your tears and put away your sadness. You only served the Great Mother's work. You did nothing wrong." The Clan Mother sighed deeply, then said, "I must seek the Great Mother's help. Please help me prepare."

"Yes, Mother… I will bring what you need, but please rest while I prepare. Anas'kala withdrew. The Clan

Mother's words at first, helped her fear fade, but now, she felt it rising again. She felt as if she was again on the rock, hiding in the shadows, wondering if she were about to destroy them all.

####

Mokolo and his friend sat with their backs against the rock wall. The mid-day sun had warmed it and it felt good, easing the remaining soreness from the hunt and from cutting all the saplings down, then hauling them up to their work space. They hoped the Clan Mother would not be disappointed.

Nearby lay the sturdy litter that would carry the Clan Mother and her sacred belongings to their new home. Mokolo was filled with dread and the work barely softened his worries. The trip would be long and there would be many dangers. Maybe even bears. He knew they would have to fight for a home wherever they were going. The Clan Mother seemed to know where they were headed, though. In her raspy voice she told them she had seen it all in her dreams. The Great Mother had shown her the way. She told them their new home would be near the edge of water that never froze in winter.

"What kind of water never freezes?"Baaktolo asked him, "Is she speaking of real water, or some kind of spirit water? Magic?"

Mokolo shook his head. "I can't say. It's confusing and besides..." he leaned closer, whispering, "I don't want to leave our valley. I love it here, don't you?"

Baaktolo looked around to make sure no one was nearby, then replied, "Of course. It's all we've ever known and it has given us a good life, but... but there are the other men. They are coming and we must find a new home. That's what she said."

"I know, I heard her, but… but why can't *THEY* be the ones to leave? Why can't we keep our home? They have their own homes down at the end of that lake, why do they need our valley, too?"

Baaktolo agreed that it wasn't right at all. He whispered, "but what really scares me is… I wonder why the Great Mother…" He looked up at the clouds overhead, "…why She would let them take it all from us. Doesn't She love us?" His hand rested on his chest. He knew these were troublesome words. They might bring evil on the Clan if anyone heard them.

"I don't know. Maybe She loves the other men more." Mokolo drew his eyes down into a deep frown, then added, "If I could, I'd kill them all… even their children, then we could stay in peace, in our home. I'd fill their bodies with the feathered small spears until the valley was red with their blood."

Baaktolo rubbed his lame leg, and replied, "If I could, I'd stand beside you and kill a few myself. I'm afraid, but I'm so angry it doesn't matter."

Mokolo lay his hand upon his friend's shoulder. "We mustn't think like this. There are more of them. Many more, and they will kill all of us. It will be the end of the Clan, the end of our people. No, Baaktolo, we'll leave in the night of the new moon, just as our Mother has told us. By the time the Other men find our home, here above the Valley, we will all be far away."

"I know you're right, I just don't feel like I want to sneak away, but… well, She has spoken, and we must follow her vision."

Mokolo rose and helped his friend up as well, they each took one of the long side-poles of the litter they had lashed together with rawhide strips, then raised it up and leaned the entire frame against the rock face. At its base lay more saplings, their bark peeled and their surfaces scraped smooth. These were to become bearing poles for the many bundles that would need to come with them on the journey. Mokolo pushed against the litter from one side to test how rigid it was and whether it could withstand the rugged path ahead. He knew the Clan Mother was not small or light in weight. And she would also carry her sacred items. It had to last the whole journey. Four hunters had been selected as carriers; but first, the litter must be finished with the bearskins and the deerskin bags. It must be woven back and forth across almost its whole length, with more deerskin rawhide, then the skins must be sewn into place.

Baaktolo had been notching small saplings and stripping out lengths of raw deerskin for many days now. The results were rough looking. Nothing like his beautifully decorated gourds or the other things he made, but it would have to do. Far off, high above the river, Mokolo watched a pair of hawks gliding in the breezes and updrafts. *If only I could fly*, he thought. *Then no one would ever be able to make me leave my home.*

Chapter 29

The morning air was crisp and the sky clear. Anson had just climbed down from the roof of the watch outpost. His watch was over, and he entered the cabin to quench his thirst and maybe grab a bite of dried meat. Not much talk this morning, he noted. Just as well. He wanted to conserve his energy. He had a long way to go before nightfall.

"Anson!" Nils voice boomed out from the shadows across the fire pit.

"Nils! I didn't see you there. Are you joining today's watch?"

"No, not today." Nils stood up and joined Anson by the door. Anson tried to hide his disappointment that he'd been caught. By Nils, no less. He hoped whatever the chief had in mind would not take long. He needed some sleep before traveling. Nils continued, "But, I'd like to speak with you as you return home..."

"Of course, Nils. I'd just like to drink some water and grab something to eat. It won't be a moment."

Anson moved fast to secure the dipping gourd and grab a few morsels of dried meat and then returned, his kit upon his back. "So, shall we leave?"

He stuffed the meat into his mouth and began chewing as they left the outpost. He tried to set a quick pace. After they were some distance off, Nils began with a question. "I spoke with the Seer yesterday. He mentioned he hadn't heard from you in maybe ten days. He seemed concerned. Is all well with your daughter? Uhhh... Gunda?"

"Oh yes, she is fully recovered now, as fit as ever. I've... I've been so busy working inside, and planning the hunts and all I guess I just forgot to make time to sit with the Seer. I may be able to see him tomorrow, though."

"Well, I told him you were on watch until this morning. He said he'd put time aside for you as you returned home. I'm sure you can make time for him this morning, can't you?"

"Yes, I suppose I can" Anson's mind reeled. This was not the good start he'd hoped for. Who knew what the Seer wanted or how long it would take. His wife had everything ready. The frame for Gunda to ride upon her father's back was padded and covered with a new deerskin from the last hunt. She had packed dried meat, nuts and dried fruit for many days and there were four water gourds at the ready.

"Good. As the time approaches for you to lead the hunters into the high valley to … to rout the trolls there, we will need the Seer's words and visions, more and more. When did you say the time would be right?"

"We are ten, no eleven days from the dark of the moon. I want to travel under a dark moon for the first nights, to keep our progress hidden. So, it will be eleven days."

"I see… and does the Seer agree?"

"I don't know that I spoke to him about it. I have been planning the hunt times for a long while now, and didn't think it mattered if the Seer agreed." Anson tried to pick up the pace, but as they spoke, Nils seemed to be lagging a bit. Slowing them down with each step.

"Well then you can speak with him about it today, when you see him. I'll be speaking with him again in two days' time on another matter. It's good that you get his blessing on your departure plans. He knows the troll stories. He knows what you will be dealing with."

Anson nodded, replying, "I'll be sure to discuss it with him… today." He hoped that would settle it with Nils, and also hoped Nils would not want to talk the whole way back, but, in fact, he wanted to discuss the recovery of another hunter who had been ill after being injured in

144

the last hunt. Nils wanted him to accompany them to the high valley, and was glad he'd have more time to mend. They covered the last of the lake-side path and approached the gate in the palisade of logs erected around the village. Nils clapped him on the shoulder as they separated, saying, "Give my regards to your wife and family. We'll speak again before you leave."

That shook Anson. He replied, "Leave?"

"Leave on the high valley hunt, of course!" Nils called out as he strode away towards his home. Anson was worried. No one could know. He clenched his teeth and turned towards the path to the Seer's home... *more like a lair*, he thought wrinkling up his nose as he remembered the smell inside.

"And how is... your little Gunda, Anson?" The Seer seemed to be troubled today, Anson noted. His eyes burned with something... something Anson couldn't really explain.

"She's feeling much better, she's... she is almost completely well." Anson remembered what Gudrun was planning to say if she was asked where he had gone. He had been about to say Gunda was well, but thought better of it.

"I'm glad she has showed no signs of troll magic, has she?"

"Troll magic?" This was something Anson hadn't heard before. *What game was the Seer playing with him?* "I did not know trolls were... magical, Seer."

"Those flowers the troll gave Gunda – have you ever seen them before? Have you ever heard of them before?"

"Well, not really, but there are many things I'm sure I have not seen before. It is a very big world, isn't it?"

"Yes, but surely you can understand my concern. What if those flowers were somehow... changed. Made to work one way for Gunda, and poison anyone else who ate them? What if the trolls know the dark ways of poisons?

Did you think of that?" The Seer's voice grew in volume as he spoke, the words running into each other in their haste to leave his lips. Anson tried to hide the fear he felt spreading from this ungainly, dark and smelly man.

"They just seemed like flowers to me... why, I ate one myself, just to make sure. The trolls... they seemed just like other men, only different looking. Maybe they have a different kind of healing that works for them, and also might work for us?" As soon as the words left his lips, Anson felt a chill. He'd said too much. He could see the Seer withdrawing and reacting to his words by growing darker, if that was possible. The smells swimming in the air inside the Seer's hovel didn't help.

"Anson, what do you know of magic, of changing, of dark things? You are a hunter. You know nothing of those arts and the dark skills."

"You are right, Seer. I know nothing of those things." He hoped that would settle it.

"Still, your daughter is recovering, and you... you cling to the belief that the trolls red flowers cured her... don't you?" The Seer's eyes flashed like lightning bolts. They burned into his own eyes so much they made Anson's eyes begin to water.

"I had thought that. Was I wrong to think that?"

"Yes. You were wrong. I believe those flowers were a means to lure us to them. To lure our children and then take them and do unspeakable things with them... even eat them! Did you know that trolls are known to have eaten children, Anson?"

Anson shook his head. In his mind, he again saw the troll girl, kneeling, speaking softly to him, offering her cure to his stricken child. Eat children? He could not believe that. He didn't care what the Seer said, it was not true. It was a story, made up by frightened people, that was all it was.

"Well they do!" Now the Seer was almost shouting. "Mind this and mind your hunting party when you venture into that valley. When are you planning to go?"

"I want to leave at the dark of the moon, for cover."

The Seer seemed to mull his over for a while, rubbing his chin with his fist, as if that would suddenly sprout a new thought or idea. Finally, he said, "Good. That is soon enough. Be sure to see me once more before you go. I will have called for visions and will bless all of you in your hunt. I hope, for the sake of all our children, that you force the trolls away... or kill them all, if that is possible." The Seer stood. Anson realized thankfully, that his session was now over and he could return home to find sleep and prepare for his quiet departure in the shadows after night had fallen. He rose, and clapped his chest and thanked the Seer for his wisdom, still wondering what the Seer was so afraid of. Magic poison flowers, indeed! What foolishness.

\# \# \# \#

Gudrun's eyes were filled with tears. She clung to Anson as Gunda's little hands petted her mother's hair from her perch atop her father's shoulders. "Promise me, you'll be home in eight days. Both of you."

"I promise, Gudrun."

"Me, too...I promise, too!" shouted little Gunda, not to be forgotten.

Gudrun kissed Anson as he lifted the last bag and slung it over his neck and shoulder. He looked ridiculous, bulging awkwardly in every direction with his burdens lashed to every available space. He knelt down so that Gudrun could also kiss her daughter, then rose and gave his remaining children a group hug. "We must be away before they close the gates."

Gudrun watched them walk away for a time, until only the silhouette of a very tall, wide man with a tiny head could be seen as they passed from her sight, behind one of the large trees in the common grounds.

"Don't worry, Mother… Father is strong and smart and they'll be fine." Haakon stood at his mother's side, laying his hand upon her arm to comfort her. He was the man of the house for now, but when she looked down at him, his lip was quivering and his eyes were swimming with tears.

Anson and Gunda slipped through the gate as soon as they noticed the gatekeepers' attention was on their game of tossed bones near their small fire. Both of their backs were facing the open gate. Anson thought to himself as he slipped silently by them in the dark, that he'd have to mention that to Nils on his return.

Gunda looked up watching the clouds run away, revealing more stars than she thought she'd ever seen. She almost cried out in joy, but remembered her father's stern warning against speaking while they were on the move unless she saw danger. She kept still as he strode over the rough ground, swaying back and forth with his steps until the motion lulled her to sleep. Their path led up and over the hill that the outpost was on, but well back from it, in the woods. Anson knew the game trails they would follow as well as the path to his door. There was enough light from the waning moon to guide them even when the trees closed above them. He made sure that they would pass the outpost and its watchers far off, in the trees along one particular path that led away and towards the Falls, above the lake.

There was a ford he knew well, where the river ran shallow over a bed of soft gravel that they would use to cross and head up towards the high valley on the far side of the narrow part of the lake. They made no sound when at last they passed the outpost in the darkness. Anson saw

the soft orange glow of light spilling from the door flap
when he looked back, safely past a point where they could
be seen by a sharp pair of eyes. He thought how strange to
be sneaking past my fellows. The soft orange glow
disappeared all too soon. It had given him, he realized,
some small comfort, but no comfort awaited them where
they were heading.

Chapter 30

"Father? Did you hear that?" Gunda's voice, filled with alarm, was just a whisper.

"Yes, Gunda. I heard it. We will wait a bit, here before continuing on." He reached up and patted her hands where they were joined over his breastbone.

They found a rock they could sit on behind a group of bushes that gave them low cover and waited for more sounds of rocks falling. Anson knew the sound well. There was a talus slope up above them, where the rocky ridge met the forest. Along it were several large rock outcroppings where deer would graze the lichen that grew on the rocks. The leathery plant was very salty, and when hunting, he knew this was a good spot to wait for the sounds of their hooves slipping on loose rock. In a few moments, the sound came again, fainter. He relaxed a bit. He knew a predator would not have made the same mistake twice. He rose, using his spear to pull himself up off the rock. It had served as a good walking staff. He was surprisingly tired. She weighed much less than even a good-sized deer haunch, but still, as they walked off the distance, he was feeling her added weight. His step had much less spring than he was used to on a hunt, and so he made up for it by moving cautiously.

After they'd walked a while, he heard her breathing deepen and slow. He knew she was asleep. The thought took him to his warm bed, to his hearth near where the rest of his children and his beloved Gudrun slept peacefully, he hoped. He had to work to crowd the thought away before he began to doubt he was doing the right thing. He might be a fool, or an idiot, but there was no time for that now. They had to get at least to the path that climbed up next to the falls and into the high valley, where he knew a huge tree waited to give them a night's shelter.

They were walking along a game trail that ran just inside the woods, along the creek that flowed into the lake, further down. The gentle rippling sounds were a reminder of his days exploring, along with his chums, when he was a boy. He smiled as he walked, swinging his spear along with each step, the extra bags bobbing against his legs. Far off, ahead, he heard an owl calling to its mate in the darkness. A harsh, crying scream, it would be frightening to someone who wasn't so familiar with the call of this kind of female owl. He was glad Gunda still slept on. There were more night calls and noises in the woods as the darkness deepened, but none were alarming. They were the sounds Anson knew as the sounds of those animals and birds who shared their valley, and he felt almost friendship with them as he passed them quietly in the dark.

Just before the moon finally began to sink beneath the high trees, Anson had climbed up the trail next to the falls and entered the high valley at last. Up ahead in the darkness lay a gigantic, spreading oak whose heavy, high limbs would carry them both safely through the rest of the night. As they approached the tree he gently awakened his daughter.

"Gunda, wake. We are at our first night's resting spot." She mumbled, sleep-slurred and he patted her hands adding, "Wake Gunda! We must climb."

In a few moments, he was passing up their bags to his daughter who had climbed up as nimble as could be. She sat astride a heavy branch just above his reach, and she took them one by one: the frame she rode on, and his weapons. Last, he pushed his spear up to her, butt first. He followed, quickly after. Gunda then, climbed up to the next highest level he could still reach, and in this way, three more times, they reached a huge four-way saddle in the trunk, far above the ground. Anson settled into a well-worn spot he'd ridden the night out in several times before. He could rest, leaning back against the trunk and held on either side by stout limbs that rose from this union. It was as comfortable as a tree could be. He settled Gunda in his lap and wrapped her up in the bearskin they carried. Soon she fell asleep again, the only sounds were the far-off rush of the waterfall below them and the singing of the crickets.

The very next day, Gunda woke early and saw the sun creep over the far off ridges at the end of the lower valley. Soft tendrils of misty light seeped into the woods and through the branches that cradled them. She listened to the bird songs for a while before waking her father by stroking his face with her hand. A new day had dawned and here they were, safe high in the branches of an ancient tree. Gunda smiled as Anson opened his eyes.

She whispered, "You slept a long time, Father. See how the sun is already rising?"

"Shhh! We don't want to wake up the whole forest do we?" He was cross with himself for falling asleep at all and rubbed the grit from his eyes. His shoulders hurt and he noticed his legs had gone numb also. He retrieved the nearest bag from where it had been slung over a stub of a branch and asked Gunda quietly for one of the water gourds within her reach. He passed her one of the fruit and nut cakes Gudrun had packed for them while he took several pieces of dried meat for himself. They ate the first breakfast of their great adventure as he had called it, quietly listening to the sounds of the woods around them waking.

Soon, they were once again walking a game trail. This was one he had found leading along the creek when they had first ventured into the high valley many years before. He liked to use it because it was covered above by the trees that grew thickly near the water, but also because he could clearly see anything that might approach from across the creek. He had warned Gunda that she would

152

have to be their eyes and ears behind them as they walked, and also up into the woods at the side of the trail as they climbed up into the valley. She was happy to have a serious job and promised she would not miss anything at all.

"But remember," he told her, "don't speak loudly, even in alarm. We must pass quietly up the valley, unseen and unheard."

# # # #

Two more nights passed in the same way, in the cradles of trees, far above the ground. Anson did not sleep. The journey had taken them up, past the place where the knife lion had killed Raka. He didn't speak of it to Gunda, but it weighed on his mind. They saw many deer and other animals. Once, when they had stopped to fill their water gourds, Gunda pointed out a family of otters playing happily in the creek, sliding off the bank and onto each other in a game of tag. She had to stifle her laughter.

As they walked further, though, Anson began to feel a sense of dread. They were coming to a part of the valley he had never ventured into before. None of their people had. Fear had kept them from entering. Fear of bears. Fear of lions and fear of trolls. Now here he was, walking his daughter right into their dens. The woods on their near side began to thin and the talus slopes from the cliffs were now creeping closer. Soon, he knew, there would be much less cover. He wished he could have dodged this task. He'd tried to talk himself into forgetting the kindness of the troll girl, but he couldn't do it. If there were spirits that helped protect men who were trying to do the right thing, he wished he knew how to reach them and gain their help.

The high valley was wide and heavily treed at the end near the falls, but it narrowed considerably further up. He saw that ahead, the canyon walls almost grew together across the creek. If there were any trolls about... *other men about*, he corrected his thought: *they would be visible when they passed that point.*

A few miles later, they rested under a big spreading tree at the edge of the creek. Gunda dangled her feet in the water to cool them. She'd insisted that she could walk and he'd lost the strength to argue, but when she'd stood up to explore along the grassy banks, he'd called to her.

"No Gunda! You must stay close. One or two strides from me. We don't know what may be crouching under a bush or up in a tree, just waiting for a nice, juicy... girl to stumble along. I don't want you to be lunch for a big animal... do you?"

"Oh no! I don't!" She ran back and threw her arms around his tired shoulders. He patted her head and she returned to her place with her feet in the swirling water.

Anson looked out across the creek, to the other side. He'd been glancing in every direction every few seconds, keeping a sharp eye for movement. A short run from the creek, on the other side, were rocky cliffs that led up to jagged crags. He could just see high enough to notice several dark openings. Caves. Lairs. He called to his daughter, once again.

"Gunda, we must go. Now." She jumped up, and ran to join him. He motioned for her to lead along the game trail they'd been following. He whispered to her, "Soon, you'll need to climb up on my back again, as we pass into the gorge ahead, where the path disappears." She nodded.

After a few fleet minutes walking quickly into the cover of the trees, he knelt down and she climbed up into the carry-frame she'd been riding in. It was no longer as comfortable, or as special as it had been when they left home. No fun at all. Anson knew she wanted to walk, but she kept still as he crept around holding close to the rock face to his right while they passed into the shadows of the gorge.

Chapter 31

"They should be back in a few days' time," Gudrun told Nils, trying to keep her face calm. "He told me he knows where he can find the flowers... up near where the Seer's lookout rock is," she added.

"Did he speak with the Seer before leaving?" Nils was not pleased to hear this news. The Seer had been asking him for days now, why Anson hadn't stopped to speak with him. The last two times, he'd been more and more agitated. Nils had no idea what was going on, since it was many days until the dark of the moon and the hunting trip into the high valley. He decided to press Gudrun for more information.

"You say he took your daughter with him? Into the woods? That seems an odd thing for a father to do."

Gudrun tried to remain unconcerned, keeping her reply light and easy, "Yes, he said there would be no danger, and that way... Gunda would be able to begin eating the flowers right away and not have to wait for him to return home."

"I see... so you have no worries? Is there anything I can do while he is gone to help you and your children?"

"No, thank you Nils, but I can't think of anything. He made sure we had firewood and meat to last, and our small garden is right behind the house." Gudrun smiled and hoped it had been enough to satisfy Nils. This had been the second time he'd asked about Anson's departure. She swallowed her building fear and said, "I'll be sure to send him to you as soon as they return."

Nils slapped his chest and left their door, walking very quickly. She watched him until he was out of sight behind another house, then she sat down on the log by the door to wonder why the Seer was so upset. Could it be as Anson had confided, that the Seer fears for his position in the village, in the case that a greater healer might step forward? Was there anything Anson had kept from her? She didn't think so, but she decided to keep her children close until Anson and Gunda returned. She had never liked the Seer. He smelled bad, and his eyes were always wandering.

# # # #

"He took his daughter with him? Are you sure of this?" The Seer rose to his feet and grasped both of Nils' arms in surprise.

Nils nodded. "That is what his wife has told me twice now. It is hard to believe, but he knows the slopes above your high lookout quite well, in fact, we both hunted it so thoroughly that I'd be surprised if he even saw a rat or a squirrel. There's little to fear up there... unless you have seen..."

The Seer almost told Nils that trolls had been seen there, but held his tongue. Better to control how this got out. He relaxed and let his hands fall from Nils arms. He saw red finger marks left in the flesh, and apologized to Nils. "I'm sorry I gripped you so hard – I was just so surprised... I didn't really think."

"It's no worry at all. I just wanted to let you know where Anson had gone, since you were asking for him. But let me ask again, have you seen? Is there something he should fear? We should fear?"

The Seer rolled his eyes back into his head, and raised his chin. It had always been a useful trick, when he needed a moment to collect his thoughts. He wanted to convey some new fear, but not enough to send a hunting party after Anson. Not yet, at least. He slowly shook his head from side to side, then spoke, "Yes. I have dreamt of trolls again. Trolls moving down over the falls, with many spears, yet there has been nothing sighted from the outpost. I am worried they may have ways to move we know nothing about. There may be secret caves, secret paths only they know, so we must watch carefully until Anson returns and we can move our hunters against them."

"Yes, but should we send a party to track Anson and bring him home?"

There it was. "No, we should remain here. He is safe enough up where his wife said he was headed. We'll see both of them soon, I'm sure." Nils nodded. It seemed to satisfy him, and he took his leave. The Seer watched him until he disappeared into the village, then returned to his smoky fire. *This would not do*, he thought. He'd been up early gathering herbs every day for many days now. He'd seen no one leave the village and turn up to the path towards the lookout rock. *He would have seen.* He was sure. *Why would Anson's wife lie to Nils? Where was Anson?* The Seer ground his fist into his open palm. This would not do at all. He reached over towards the fire, where a small basket held a bundle of herbs. He picked it up, stripping off half of it and threw it on the fire where it began to smolder, filling the dark hovel with an even more disgusting smell and choking smoke. He inhaled deeply, and thought, *we'll see. We'll see.*

After three more days, and no sign of Anson, the Seer could let it rest no longer. He was convinced he could persuade the village that trolls had captured Anson and Gunda. A rescue party would be mustered. He stepped out into the mid-morning light and grimaced as his eyes adjusted. Far off, up the lake, he looked hard, trying to focus enough to see the falls, but it didn't matter, he knew they were there, and soon enough, Nils would lead them there and higher, into the lair of the trolls. *We will kill every one*, he decided, smiling, *every last one.* He grabbed his staff and strode off to speak with Nils.

"... so you see... we just don't have any choice, now. We'll rescue Anson and his little daughter and put an end to the trolls' evil."

Nils rubbed his bearded chin, thoughtfully, absorbing the Seer's alarming story. What else, could they do? He asked the Seer to tell the whole village what had come to him in dreams, especially the warning about the dark of the moon.

"I saw a vision of the trolls creeping along a mountain pathway, close by one of our men. They were carrying the cruel black spears, and passed so close that he could have reached out with his hand to brush their dirty hides, but he couldn't see them at all. They passed him, silently, unseen... and then, next I saw them carrying off our children in the midday sun! None of our men could see them at all, and our children's cries confused and struck terror into the hearts of their mother men and fathers alike. None were left behind." The Seer paused, to let this last part sink in, then added, "All were taken away."

"And in your vision, none of us could lift a hand to stop them?" Nils had already asked this once before. He knew he had to be cautious. It would mean a large party and only a few old men would remain behind to protect the families.

"NO. No one could see them. The moon's darkness covered them and men's eyes could not see. We must strike now, before the moon is fully dark."

"I agree. I will call a council fire, and all will come to hear your dreams."

Towards evening, they came in family groups, pairs and one by one until the entire council circle was filled, with children ringing the circle. After Nils explained the need for the council, the Seer rose slowly. He stepped to where Nils was standing and began to speak of his visions, first the troll stories, finally Anson's plight and the final vision of the dark of the moon. As he croaked out

159

the tale, all voices were hushed but for the sound of some of the younger children, who now frightened by the evil story, began crying softly. Finally the Seer finished, with a call to all men to depart at first light to save Anson and his daughter from the trolls' evil hands.

A few men began shouting for blood, soon many joined in. They felt their blood lust rising, and began chanting, "Kill them all! Kill them all!" The Seer could not have asked for more. He was almost overcome at how his plans were coming to fruition and was unable to stifle a dark smile. The light began to fade and by the time the big fire was blazing in the council circle, every man was on his feet. They shook their knives in the air and screamed for the death of all trolls. Nils chose a young hunter to lead them, but the Seer stepped up again, shaking his head. "No, Nils. You must lead us!"

The angry crowd took up a chant. "Nils! Nils! Nils Must Lead Us!" Nils spread his arms wide, then raised them both up and the voices ended. He looked around the circle and saw his village, all his relations, all his brother men and sisters. How could he refuse them? He cried, "Yes, I will lead you!"

The young man who Nils had chosen to lead was a bit deflated, but he stood with the rest, then he suddenly yelled, "Seer! Seer! Seer shall lead us!" The men took up the chant until the Seer rose again from his place near the fire. He spread his arms, then raised them and the men grew quiet. In his thick, gravelly voice, he nodded and replied, "Yes, I will go with you! I must wash your knives, your spears and the tips of your arrows in a special medicine to bless their strength. Tomorrow!" A swelling cry went up. The men's eyes glistened in the firelight as they began stomping their feet in unison and chanting "Kill them all! Kill them all! Kill them all!"

After speaking again with Nils, when the council fire died down to embers, the Seer sat near his own fire. He was adding hot rocks from his hearth to a large bubbling water basket holding a special combination of Hemlock and the tops of select mushrooms, along with a few other ingredients. The resulting poison would kill. Maybe not right away, but it would kill surely, any whose skin was pierced. Even trolls, he hoped. He'd bring it to the gate tomorrow as a "blessing" on their hunt and the rescue of Anson and his daughter. They would immerse the tips of their weapons and he would leave with the hunting party, but he was also sure that some ailment would stop him before he made it over the falls.

He would be forced to return to the village, and while he would say he wished he were able to continue with them, he'd count on cautious old Nils to insist that the stricken Seer return home. Exactly according to plan.

Chapter 32

Anson felt a sudden chill as he followed the tiny
game trail around the blind corner into the shadows of the
cliffs. They towered over his head, to his right, and were
almost as high across the creek. Rock ledges jutted out
above him, and he knew he had to move fast if he didn't
want to be seen from any number of good vantage points
he'd seen as he crept through the shadows. Ahead, the
brush began growing again as soon as the shadows gave
way to sunlight, but even that was pitiful cover. He picked
up the pace and whispered to Gunda to be still. He saw no
movement anywhere on either side and heard nothing.
Odd, he thought as he walked, not even the songs of birds.

Ahead, closer to the uplands, with ledge after ledge
rising above them in terraced slopes, stood a huge oak
tree, its branches straining upwards to catch as much light
as it could. It was very thickly surrounded by heavy brush
as well, and he saw in an instant it would make a good
destination for the night. The game trail wound back into
the trees so that their cover had improved from above, but
they could still be seen from the slopes above them on the
creek side, so he moved quickly. Soon, they approached
the tree, and he noticed with satisfaction that across the
creek, the uplands and rock ridges were further back,
away from the creek.

Directly across the water was a tall stand of reeds,
and he shuddered, remembering how they had come upon
a troll or trolls in reeds just like these but further back,
closer to the falls. He watched the tops of the reeds closely
for a time, from behind a large boulder with a thorn bush
growing from under it, but saw no movement. There was
little breeze, and he was glad their scent would remain
close to them. He told Gunda that they would wait for
darkness to climb up for the night, and pointed at a large
junction of several heavy branches where they would be

able to rest. She nodded and began to glance around, just like her father, scanning every direction for movement of an unnaturally-occurring darkness in the foliage. He smiled. Gunda was learning the skills of a tracker. She'd never really have to use them though because she was just a woman, she'd never be a hunter. He passed her some of the last meat from his pouch, and a few dried berries. It would have to do for now. They were almost at the end of the valley, where high rocky ridges closed the space. He could see a tiny silver thread where the creek came over in one last sparkling fall before continuing on the valley floor.

As they waited for the sun to fall behind the ridges at the end of the valley, Anson went over and over in his mind what he would say and do when they were seen, or when they saw the... other men. He would raise both hands up, then fall to his knees, laying his bow and arrows and spear out on the ground in front of him, and extend his arms towards the other men, palms up, the way the troll girl had done. He had explained to Gunda that she also should do exactly as he did. He hoped they would understand that he would do them no harm. He thought they might think he needed help.

Later that night, after climbing up higher than they had previous nights, Anson and Gunda were sleeping. Suddenly, they were awakened by the sharp scream of a lion nearby. It sounded like it was on the same limb! Anson wiped his eyes clean, and tried to hear small movements. He touched Gunda and put his finger on her lips to keep her quiet. After a few tense moments, he heard a scuttling sound through the brush directly below them, then a crashing noise as what must have been a deer, sprang through the brush and ran off a full speed towards the creek.

A second crash followed as the deer was pursued by what Anson thought must have been the lion, but he wondered why it had screamed and alerted the deer? Then it came to him: *maybe it was another lion that had screamed.* He tensed up, in full alert now, waiting, keeping his breathing slow and full but quiet so he could hear everything. It was then that he smelled the smoke. There was little light from the moon, as it slid behind cloud after cloud.

Carefully pushing branches aside, to reveal sight-lines in each direction, he finally caught sight of the flicker of a fire nearby. Then came a shout. Then a reply shout from the direction of the fire. They'd practically stumbled into a hunting camp! But why were they hunting at night? Then he realized that the second crash he'd heard, and the sound of pursuit had probably been a hunter, not a lion. He was glad he'd been asleep. He might have moved or done something to give away their position above the game trail, and when he finally came upon the... other men, he didn't want it to happen in darkness. There were shuffling and crunching sounds, like heavy footfalls all night long. He was grateful for the little sleep he'd gotten before they were awakened. The moon remained hidden the rest of the night, and by morning, both Anson and Gunda had fallen asleep again, high above the ground in the embrace of the oak tree.

Light was just beginning to peek through the leaves when Anson was awakened by a hollow thumping sound that seemed to come from the trunk of the tree itself. He quickly blinked away the grit in his eyes and saw that Gunda was intently watching something going on far below them on the ground. Looking down, Anson saw a large, very hairy troll... man, thumping the butt of his spear against the trunk of the tree they were in. Anson watched in mounting horror, waiting for the man to look up through the branches and see their feet hanging down, but he just kept thumping. Finally, he looked carefully at the end of his spear, where the thumping had rounded it off, and walked away.

Anson exhaled in relief, very slowly. Gunda was trying to reach his arm to alert him, so he caught her hand and smiled, wiping off his brow to indicate his relief, but then as he looked at her, he realized his relief was to be short lived. They were at, or close to their destination. Only close to a man's home would he risk hunting in darkness. He carefully removed the last of the food from his pouch, swallowed a small mouthful of water from the gourd and passed most of the meat, acorn cakes and berries to Gunda along with the water gourd.

After they had eaten, Anson very slowly, very deliberately climbed down a few branches, then looked all around, in every direction to be sure they were not seen. He'd wait a while, then continue down a few more, until he was an easy jump off the ground. Below the tree there were many marks in the disturbed soil and along the game trail, both deer tracks and footprints. Men had come this way. He saw a line cutting through the tall grass which showed where the deer had run with the hunter close behind him. Looking back away from the creek, he saw the reason the deer had been caught. Protruding from the nearest rock outcropping was a large white crust of salt. The deer came here to lick the salt, so of course, hungry hunters knew where to find them. He rapped the tree trunk twice with his spear to alert Gunda, who began climbing down herself. He wanted to take a moment to show her the salt and explain what had happened in the darkness. Soon, they were standing near the salt lick.

As Anson whispered to Gunda about deer and salt and hunting, she touched his arm and pointed to a slight movement in a dense clump of low brush very close by the outcropping. Together they crept up close. When they peered inside, they saw a tiny, very frightened fawn, crouching on its knees, trying to hide itself until its mother

returned. Anson knew she would not return. An unlikely
feeling swept over him. He wanted to protect the
quivering baby deer. He knew it was useless. He knew it
would fight him and probably run anyway, eventually to
make a meal for some predator, still… he wanted to try.
He quietly unslung the carry frame upon his back, and
leaned it against the rock, then crept up quietly and very
slowly, until he was close enough to make a sudden lunge
through the brush and grab the fawn.

It bawled, louder than he expected, and struggled
fiercely, nipping him with tiny teeth and trying to kick
him. He grabbed its ankles, and covered it with his body,
then, pulling out the long cord, he hobbled its legs.
Finally, the fawn rested, panting on its side in the grass, its
feet tied together. Gunda jumped up and down and asked
her father what he was going to do.

"You won't hurt it will you? It's just a baby!" Gunda
started to cry.

Anson quickly whispered, "No, don't cry. We'll just
take it with us."

Gunda smiled, and in a few minutes after each of
them had made water and they were ready, watched in
awe as her father slung the fawn up, over his head, to ride
across his shoulders, its legs lying on his chest. After a
few feeble cries and attempts to struggle, it lay there, still,
with its head down, lying atop Anson's shoulder. Anson
slung his bow over his neck and shoulder, then his pouch
and his arrows, and handing Gunda the water gourd, they
started up the trail. Gunda whispered, pointing back, "But
what about the carry-thing I ride on?"

Anson wondered how to explain leaving it, then said,
simply, "We won't be needing it anymore." It leaned
there, against the rock outcropping where he'd left it.
Anson figured that if it was there when they made their
way home, he'd pick it up. He pointed to the trail, and

with Gunda leading, they quietly made their way towards
their encounter with the other men.

Chapter 33

Mokolo saw his reflection shining back at him from
the deep stone cistern inside the cave. He'd crept back at
first light, to help the water keeper bring up the morning's
water, but really, to see if he might meet Anas'kala as she
rose. He had much to say to her as the time of their first
lying approached. He smiled at his own silly face smiling
back at him in the dark water when the Water Mother
thrust her gourd into the middle of the reflection to begin
filling her water basket. He backed away, in deference and
asked if he might help carry the water back to the cooking
fire. She nodded, then replied, "I'm sure I don't know
why a strong hunter would want to spend his time with
this old woman."

"I… I just wanted to be helpful, Mother."

"And, I suppose, you had no other reason to be here,
so close to where another woman might be rising?"

Oh… not really, no." Mokolo felt his face blush as
her true meaning sunk in.

He lifted the heavy basket when it was filled, and
carried it back towards the mouth of the cave near the
cooking fire, where he sat it down, looking over his
shoulder, for Anas'kala to appear. He drifted back towards
the cistern. He wasn't hungry at all. At yesterday's return,
the hunters had brought back two large fourlegs. One had
been his alone. He had the idea to creep up to the salt lick
and surprise one before the dawn came. He had gotten the
surprise, though. While he was hiding under a big tree, a
lion screamed close by and he almost lost his prey. It was
spooked by the cat's cry and lunged over a bush, but
Mokolo had been able to follow and kill it quickly with a
single spear thrust. He carried it back, proudly, Datolo
walking with him. Everyone shared a great, joyous feast.
Datolo had spent some time with him after they had
stuffed their bellies almost to bursting.

Mokolo remembered they spoke of the hunt, and his crazy idea of hunting at night, alone. Datolo said he never expected it to work. "We heard the cat scream, and we figured you were gone. Lion food. When you came scrambling back into camp, you were the last person I thought I'd see, do you remember my face?"

"Mokolo laughed aloud, replying "You looked like you'd seen a bear walking into camp with me."

"And when you said you had a fourlegs, just outside the fire... what did I look like then?"

"Mokolo thought about it, then told him, "Your smile was so big, I worried your ears would fall into your mouth!"

"You did well, Mokolo – took a risk, but it was clear thinking. Next time, though, take a few of us with you."

"I will, Chief. I will."

Datolo changed the subject. "Have you felt your seed quickening? Soon you will lie with a woman."

"I... I guess so. My spear grows large all the time now." Mokolo remembered his embarrassment when, during the return, with a carry-pole upon his shoulder, his man-spear had suddenly grown so large it caught everyone's attention. It couldn't be hidden. One of his friends, laughed and said, "Looks like Mokolo has another fourlegs in his mind... or is it a twolegs?" Everyone laughed and pointed, and he tried to cover himself with his free hand, but it did no good, then it subsided as the rest finally quit making fun of him. Still, he knew it was funny.

He smiled thinking of it, but soon his thoughts had drifted back to Anas'kala and what awaited them as they prepared to leave their home. The excitement of their coming coupling faded to a dull ache as he watched the water in the cistern turn still and very dark.

# # # #

169

Anas'kala crept up next to the Clan Mother's bed, and waited. The Clan Mother was moving slower than ever and it was worrying the girl. She also heard the Clan Mother grunt and moan in the darkness as even this movement was causing her pain. For the past three moon cycles, she had tried to absorb all the lessons her grandmother had been trying to teach her, but she was afraid she would forget something really important. The Clan Mother also wanted her to join with Mokolo and receive his seed before the dark of the moon. Everything was approaching too fast and that troubled her, too.

The Clan Mother returned, and with a sigh, heaved her large body up onto her bearskin bed. "Come here, my daughter's daughter... I need to speak with you about lying with a man." Anas'kala extended her hand to touch her grandmother's shoulder in the near darkness. "Tell me, child, what you know about it."

Anas'kala wondered where to start, so she quietly asked, "Where do I begin, Mother?"

"Tell me how to begin lying with a man to accept his seed."

"Well... I touch his spear, very gently. I run my fingers down and up and down again along it, until I feel it come to life. I heard that it will get very big, and hard, too, but not like rock."

"Yes, child, that is all true. Then what will you do?"

I heard I was supposed to touch the man all over his body, and brush his eyelids with my fingers. He will do the same to me, and he will touch my cleft... and when it is ready, it will be damp, then he will... he will..." Anas'kala worried about how this was supposed to happen. No one had told her.

"Do you know what you need to do, child?"

"No, Mother, I... I'm not sure, how to lie, or do I turn over, or do I stand?"

"You may find many different ways, but you will need to be comfortable, so I would have you lie on your back. He will lie between your legs and then, do you know what will happen?"

"Yes. Will it hurt much?"

"It is different for every woman, but you must try to relax at the moment he enters you, so it won't hurt as much. You may need to grip the bearskin in both hands and squeeze. It helped me."

"How many times will I need to do this until I have accepted his seed?"

"It may only need one time, or it may need many, but you will know when it has taken place."

"Will it always hurt?"

"No, after a time it will not hurt at all, in fact, you may cry out from the pleasure. So may he. Don't be afraid of any of this. It is a gift our Mother has given us all, to bring new life forth in pleasure. Your cries may be cries of joy, once you and Mokolo have lain together many times. It gets better. Do you understand?"

"I think so... will it feel like when I touch myself?"

"Maybe better, maybe not as good. It is different for everyone. My advice is to show Mokolo whatever you feel, and share yourself with him. Take of his sharing, too. There is much that will happen inside your body, but much will happen also in your heart. When it is best, it is best in both places. That is what I wish for you my daughter's daughter."

"Thank you. I will pray to the Great Mother and thank her for her many gifts." Anas'kala paused, then asked, "Have you decided which night will be our night?"

"Yes. Your night will be tomorrow night. I will send the message to the Hunt chief, and you are free, now, to speak with Mokolo. Tell him the news, and show him the special place made for you. " The Clan Mother lay her heavy hand upon her granddaughter's shoulder and squeezed gently, adding, "It has been my greatest joy to watch you grow into a woman and learn the healing arts and our clan secrets. You have made me so very proud of you. I … I only wish your mother could have seen it unfold as it has." She touched her granddaughter's face and Anas'kala backed away slowly, towards the light coming from the outer passage.

The Clan Mother wiped away a tear brought by the memory of her daughter, Anas'kala's mother, who had been injured when Anas'kala was just a very small girl. She died knowing her own mother would take her little girl to her heart, too. Now the little girl would soon carry the seed of a man and create life inside her. Soon, she would lead the clan to their new home. Anas'kala would make the trip, but she herself? The Clan Mother knew her time was now very short. She would not have the strength to travel, but she didn't want to tell everyone. They needed to keep her strength and wisdom in their hearts. She would carry on until her last breath fled. She hoped they had the time to lay her among her family for her slumber, before they left the valley for good.

Chapter 34

"I'm only telling you these things because your own father didn't live to do so. Have you understood?"

Mokolo nodded, a frown on his face. Everything Datolo had told him he'd heard bits and pieces of as he grew up, but never everything. It excited him, but it also frightened him. He asked the Hunt Chief, "You tell me that I will lie on top, but won't I hurt her? Will she feel that I have not shown her proper respect?"

"In this one way, when you bring your seed, you and your woman will be equal – the same. Neither should demand respect: both should give it. So you understand? You will be sharing each other in body and in heart. It will be secret, between the two of you, for evermore, and you will hold it in your heart for strength and happiness. This is a great gift of the Great Mother, that she makes bringing life forth so much joy. When you feel that joy, touching yourself, it is only half as much joy as you will feel with Anas'kala and even all that will be less than you will feel when she is bringing your child into the world, into our clan." Datolo lay his hand upon Mokolo's shoulder and added, "You would have made your father so proud. You are a good man and you will be a good father."

"Thank... thank you, Chief. I hope I do it all the right way."

"Trust me, Mokolo, the right way will be easy. You will help each other. Now go find something useful to do until tomorrow night. Tonight we will sing the song of new life for you and Anas'kala. Tonight is the end of your childhood."

# # # #

Datolo watched as Mokolo walked back toward where Baaktolo was sitting, working on another carry-frame. He was happy for him, but also worried. The message from the Clan Mother, carried by one of her youngest helpers, had named the date for the joining of the two young people, but it also carried news, in secret words, he had long hoped would not come soon. The words told him that the Clan Mother would not be going with them to their new home, in fact, she would not even leave this valley. She named her granddaughter, Anas'kala s the new Clan Mother, once she had given birth, but he and the next oldest Mother, Kappala, mother to his own children, would have to lead the tribe away. Soon. Very soon. They would begin the morning after Mokolo and Anas'kala had lain together.

Later, the young messenger found him again, after the evening meal. The Clan Mother had called him, directly, to her side. He was surprised. Only women were called to her side since she was too old to give birth. He began to fill with fear. *What did this mean*

"Datolo? Are you near?"

"Yes Mother, I am here." He was still facing the faint light coming in through the entry passage. His back remained turned to her, out of respect.

"Datolo? Turn and join me. There is little time left for traditions like this. We must talk, face to face, so you understand. I am just an old woman, not so different from all the other men."

He was shocked. It was something he had never thought of. He slowly turned around and crept closer, finding his way by the growing smell of decay and evergreen boughs. Suddenly, his hands met the edge of the Clan Mother's bed. The darkness was near complete, only a slight sparkle from her eyes led him to know where she was sitting, exactly. "Mother", he said, his voice shaking, "What can you tell me?"

"Datolo, don't fear what I'm going to tell you. These things are old, as old as our people. It has been the way for us almost as long as we have been a people. There are stories, I have passed down to Anas'kala, that tell of when the first of our people came to these valleys. There were many dangers, and often we had to fight bears and lions and ...other men, to find safe homes. We were not the first people here. Did you know that?"

"No Mother, I did not know that. I always thought we were first. The songs..."

"The songs make us feel good, but they are not completely true, for when we came, there were other men who had come first. They were very large and powerful. As big as the bears, and so we feared them. But the Great Mother spoke to our hearts and theirs, and while we could not speak their tongue, we understood that they would find the deepest places, the darkest places, the hardest places to find, and there they would live, out of any contact with us. They were few, and did not make new life often. They preferred to live close to only the fourlegs and other men of the forest, not to other people. In that way, we only knew peace and once we had created our homes, we knew safety and happiness. Then..."

She coughed twice, and Datolo heard a deep, phlegmy rattle in her breath, he heard her sipping water, then she continued. "We also knew that we had to make peace with the bears and other men who killed the fourlegs for food. Once we had that, peace was what we knew. Then... then the other men came, as we had before them, but they did not want peace." She stifled another phlegmy cough then said, "When they came finally, to fight with us for our homes, we remembered the lesson we had learned from those who came before us, and we drew away from the newcomers whenever we could. Now it is our time again, to find new, safe homes for our children. It may mean wandering, but we have known wandering. It is no stranger to us." She coughed again, then asked, "Do you understand Datolo?"

"Yes, Mother. It is time again, for us to find a new home, but how should we proceed? There are many of us, but there are more of them, and their weapons are strong. Many of us will die if they pursue us."

"Do you fear them, Datolo?"

"Yes, Mother, I do. Am I wrong to fear them?"

"No, you are not wrong, but you must remember, they are also afraid of us. Why else do they hate us so? Their fear makes their thinking... broken, not complete. But our fear can help us to move swiftly and leave them signs that discourage their following us. How do you think we should do that?"

Datolo felt the Clan Mother's faith in him, and it made him feel brave. They spoke for hours, until she was too weak to continue, but they put a plan together. It was a plan that had the whole clan split into three smaller family groups and leave at different times. Datolo also suggested that for the very first time, they post sentries, within a shout of the cave path, but hidden, up high in the rocks, to watch for the Other men, in case they tried to come into the valley before the preparations were complete. The Clan Mother told him it was a good thing to do.

Finally, they spoke of how to confuse and trouble the other men when they finally got as far into the valley as the cave. It must look as though a terrible struggle had been fought. The last group would set fires and mark the walls of the cave with their hands dipped in fourlegs blood. The fire pit would be scattered, its ashes carried out and spread in hidden places. Old, used-up baskets, spears and other objects would be torn into pieces, as if by anger, and left strewn about the cave.

In the end, the Clan Mother would remain behind, and begin singing songs to the Great Mother when she heard the other men enter the cave. It would strike fear in the hearts of the other men, and give the last clan group more time to escape unnoticed. The three groups would rejoin each other in three days' time, over the mountains behind the cave, in the long valley that lay there, to begin their journey to the sun and the water that never freezes.

Datolo had argued with the Clan Mother about the last part, the part that left her alone, singing in the cave, but she said it made no difference to her. She knew she could go no further, and it was what the Great Mother had told her would be best for her children. He wanted to ask her about the water that never froze, but forgot until he had returned to the rest, gathered in the outer cave. She had told all the women to stand together on one side and the men on another side of the cave, so they could all be counted, even the children. When that was accomplished, with the number corresponding to marks upon Datolo's staff, it was almost time. Time for Mokolo and Anas'kala to join in the special bed prepared for them, in the middle passage of the cave, but first, the evening meal and the singing to create a time of joy and pleasure that all could share in, before the hardships to come.

Chapter 35

Anson and Gunda both heard the singing drifting
down from a higher place, as they walked the game path.
It was getting much wider, now, and the singing, at first,
just little faint sounds carried on the breeze, became
louder, and louder until it was clearly the sounds of many
voices, joined. The words were odd, and rapid. Anson
remembered the odd sound of the trolls' … the other's
speech and realized this meant they were close to the
home of the other men. Surely evil things did not sing. It
lifted his heart to know he had been right all along, these
were not evil enemies, they were just different people. Not
like them, but more like them than like… bears.

Gunda started to follow the melodies with a quiet
little humming and Anson almost stopped her, but realized
that there was no reason to hide now. He picked up the
pace, the baby deer still riding across his shoulders,
Gunda skipping on ahead. As the sounds increased, the
baby deer picked up its ears and lifted its head to hear
better. Gunda noticed this, and called back to her father,
"Look, the little deer wants to sing, too!"

He saw the light increase ahead, suddenly. He was
sure it was a clearing, so he slowed his pace a bit. Off to
his left there was a sudden, loud call. Off to his right,
another one replied. He stopped and called Gunda back to
him. "We'll go on together, from here. Hold my hand and
walk slowly, as I do. We will soon be with the… other
men."

"Will the troll girl be there, too? The one who helped
me get well?"

"I hope so, Gunda. Now be brave." He squeezed her
little hand and in two more steps, the forest fell away,
revealing a broad path up the side of the mountain slope.
Far above them, the singing continued until another shout

went up from both sides. The singing stopped, and a loud cry came from up above.

Anson stopped. Standing in full sunlight without cover, he felt weak, but he forced himself to remain motionless. "Don't move Gunda. They are coming." He saw movement now, on both sides, through the cover at the edge of the forest, and movement, up above them, in the thinning trees. Two large, dark, hairy men with their spears at the ready were creeping down slowly, From the forest edge came two more, stepping through the last of the brush. Their spears were also raised. Anson knew it was much too late to run. The fawn began to struggle on his shoulders. He knelt down and Gunda also knelt down. He laid his spear and his bow down on the path in front of him, and extended his hands as he had seen the troll girl... the other's young girl, do. The other men crept closer.

Now they began shouting out to him in angry tones. Questions he did not understand. Their tongue was just noises to his ears, so he remained silent, just held his hands out palms up. Waiting for the other men to close upon them. If they were to be killed, he hoped, for Gunda's sake it would be swift and clean. He wondered what had made him think he could parlay with the... trolls.

A shadow fell across his eyes then crossed his weapons lying on the ground in front of him. The other men were upon them. He gritted his teeth and waited. Little Gunda, looked up into the odd, dark faces with deep black eyes, but instead of crying out, she began to hum the song she had heard. Softly at first, then she began smiling and singing it using nonsense syllables, over and over again. One of the men knelt down directly across from them, a spear-length away, and Anson raised his eyes to meet his.

The other's face was dark, lined and weathered with a full beard and deeply set, black eyes under bushy eyebrows. He wasn't really ugly, but very different from the people Anson knew. He had a broad nose set off by high cheekbones and a wide mouth. His lips were drawn into a thin line as he spoke to Anson again and again. He had very broad shoulders, and heavily muscled arms and legs. He would be a fearsome enemy, Anson thought, and decided to try something. He said nothing, but he began to smile.

Gunda, looking up, saw her father's smile, so she began to sing louder. The other man looked up at his fellows, now gathered around them, and spoke a few words. They replied, and he looked back, directly into Anson's eyes... held them, then he, too began to smile, his broad face lighting up. He began to laugh, actually laugh, and motioned Anson and Gunda up off their knees. His fellows retrieved Anson's spear and his bow, and Anson felt another hand pull his arrows in their sheath, off his back. He still clutched the fawn's legs together, despite the tiring animal's struggles.

Anson felt a sudden lightening of his unhappy load as strong hands lifted it right off his shoulders. As it struggled, on the ground, two of them lashed its feet to one of their spears. Between them, they began carrying it up the pathway, hanging below the spear. The other man who had locked his eyes with Anson's, motioned for them to also walk up the pathway, and he called out a stream of words that were answered. Gunda kept on singing. The other man fell in behind them, his spear leveled at their backs and they slowly began ascending towards a cave mouth, looming high above the valley floor. Gunda saw it first, and pointed. "That's where we're all going!" she said, then began singing her silly song again. In this strange procession, Anson and Gunda and one exhausted fawn were led, finally, to the home of other men.

Chapter 36

"I've decided to send you back with Ulm. He will tell Anson's family the news. You will rest, regain your strength and wait for us to return." Nils voice was dark. Final. There would be no more discussion, feigned or honest. The Seer tried not to show Nils his pleasure with the decision. They would go forward, doing his bidding and risking their own safety, and he would return to the village. He began to consider the many different, very frightening stories he would tell and how it would convince the village that his vision had kept them all safe. They were only one day's journey into the valley. Ahead, where it narrowed, The Seer was sure, lay danger. He and Ulm would retreat back down the falls after he conferred his blessing and his vision upon them all.

####

"You will find and destroy them. Songs will be sung of your bravery – all of you." The Seer was quick to add, "I've seen it. The Spirits have told me they will help you. Now, Go!"

The Seer waved his staff out over the gathered hunters as Nils stood at his side. The youngest of them seemed moved by his speech, their eyes burning in the bloodlust that he'd raised among them. They all stood, then clapped their hands on their chests. Nils lay his hand upon the old man's shoulder and asked him, "Will you be able to return to the village with only one man to help you?"

"Yes, of course. Don't give it a single thought. Now lead your hunters to the troll's lair and kill them if you can."

The hunters sprang away, down the game trail at a
gentle run while the two left behind watched them
disappear into the trees. "Let's get on down the falls, "said
Ulm, "I'm not happy to linger up here." He led the Seer
back down towards the place where the high valley fell
into the lower one. The morning light fell in bright
patches among the trees and along the banks of the creek.
Ulm was sure they would reach one of the hunt shelters by
nightfall.

# # # #

The days ended before the hunters entered the
narrows. There was a confusion of large boulders that had
rolled down against the cliffs and Nils thought they could
find a defensible location for the night behind them with
the cliffs at their back. There would again, be no fire. It
was known that trolls could see in darkness as well or
better than they could in daylight and he wanted to
minimize any warning that they were approaching and not
expose the party to any unnecessary danger. There had
been no bears seen, and only the distant cry of a knife lion
to tell him there were predators about. For that he was
grateful. He pushed the thought of poor, lost Raaka out of
his mind. Dwelling on fear would not be useful. They
must move in strength and speed.

Later, in the dim light as the sun fell behind the far
ridges, he chewed his share of their dried meat and
considered the rest of the hunt. They had seen really
abundant game – groups of grazing deer and larger ones
like camels. The game had avoided the lower valley the
past few winters and winter hunting now meant many
days' travel. This valley, on the other hand, was the way
the lake valley had been when he had been a small boy,
listening to his father's stories. Full of game for the

taking. They should not return empty-handed from this "hunt".

He did not know how much further it would be to reach the trolls, but he hoped it would be soon, while the men were still filled with The Seer's words and strong enough to do what they must. He hoped that Kells had been right, that the trolls could be killed. He still had doubts. They had seen no dead troll, only the bloody spot where it had been pierced. *Enough*, he muttered to himself. He had The Seer's words, and visions to guide them. Looking around, from face to face, he saw his hunters were also resolute. Not one betrayed fear or uncertainty in their eyes or their manner. He was very proud of them. As the night fell upon them, despite his intention to keep watch, the sounds of crickets and night birds gently carried Nils to sleep, his back against a flat rock and his hands clutching his spear upon his lap.

Chapter 37

Anson and Gunda sat upon a rock near the cave's entrance while a large group of angry-looking other men argued and spoke. Anson kept trying to find a single word he could understand, but it was pointless. Gunda had more sense – she'd found a caterpillar and was singing to it as it crawled all over her hands. As he watched them shake their fists and glare at him, he felt more and more hopeless. It had been a terrible mistake. He had brought ruin on his daughter and probably the entire village as well. He glanced back towards the pathway they'd covered coming up the slope to the cave, and sure enough, the two that had first spied them had remained to stand guard. Escape was impossible.

Suddenly, Anson heard the pitch and volume of the discussion rise, then suddenly go completely silent. He saw all the other men turn their eyes into the cave and he heard the voice of a woman speaking slowly and deliberately to the men crowded around their "captives". Anson also heard another woman's voice – softer. Older. Their voices were approaching and Anson watched as the crowd of men parted as a young woman and a very, very old one walked slowly through them. On either side, the men fell to their knees and clapped their chests then extended their hands. It reminded Anson of what the young troll girl had done before sharing the red flowers. Wait! His mind was trying to form a thought. He recognized the young woman. He nudged Gunda and pointed towards where the young woman was coming directly to them from the crowd of men.

"It's... it's her! Our friend!" Gunda broke into a bright smile and began to wave both of her hands as the women approached. The old one moved so slowly, it was clear to Anson she was in pain. She also shielded her eyes against the sun. He saw that her skin was very, very white in color. As they approached, the young woman began to speak to Gunda and her father.

When they drew near, Anson noticed that all the men still knelt, and not one of them spoke. No, there was one who seemed still angry, or concerned. He was being restrained by two of his comrades. He'd pulled one of Anson's arrows from their sheath. Ansons's spear and his bow and arrows had been laid upon the ground so that the women had to step over them. The young man was pointing the arrow at Anson in an angry manner, shaking it back and forth while muttering what must have been dark words, over and over again.

The younger woman carried a deerskin which she spread out on the ground, bidding the old woman to sit upon it. Once she was resting, the younger woman walked right up to them, then knelt down herself, extending her hands, palms up, as she had before. Anson did likewise, then gulped as he saw Gunda lean over, then touch the other woman's hands. The woman smiled, and touched Gundfa's forehead. Gunda nodded and said, "Thank you! Thank you! You made me well!"

The woman replied in her tongue, then picked up one of the long braids Gunda wore spilling down her chest. It was yellow-gold and it shone like the sun.

####

"See here! This is the same father and young girl child I gave the healing flowers to! See them! They mean us no harm!" Anas'kala lifted up the golden braid, marveling at its beauty and at the blue eyes of the girl. Seeing her full of health and strength made her happy. As the Mother had said, she had done the right thing, after all. Anask'ala turned to the Clan Mother behind her and saw that her ancient grandmother was smiling, too. "What do you think Mother? Why have they come to us?"

185

"It is a sign from the Great Mother herself," replied the Clan Mother, in a soft voice. She stopped between words to catch her breath, then added, "I believe he wanted to thank you for saving his daughter's life." She looked into his eyes to make sure and for a moment, thought she saw agreement there. "These are people from the low valley, near the lake," she called out to the rest of the clan, now huddled together behind them.

Many nodded their heads, but none had dared to creep closer, waiting, Anson saw, for the ancient woman to give them permission, it seemed. He decided she must be their healer, or even their leader. He shook his head, thinking, *no, a woman could not lead a people. Only a man can lead.* It confused him, yet the deference she was showed by even the strongest men gave him doubt.

Anask'ala spoke again to Gunda and made motion for her to stand. She wanted to take her to the Clan Mother, for her blessing. She asked Anson, but he didn't seem to understand, so she touched Gunda, then made motion indicating walking towards the Clan Mother seated only a few steps away. He suddenly smiled and nodded. She touched Gunda, then pointed to the Clan Mother, raising her heavy eyebrows. Gunda smiled, but first, looked back to her father, asking "Can I go see the old woman?"

"Yes, please show her respect. I think she is very important to these people."

Gunda began to laugh, saying "You said a joke! You called trolls people!"

"Yes, Gunda, but it is not a joke. They are people. They are just a different kind of people."

Anas'kala gently led Gunda by the hand. The Clan Mother put up her hands to receive the child, smiling a big toothless grin. Gunda smiled, too and touched the old woman's hands before sitting at her feet. Gunda was trying not to notice how big and twisted they were, but she felt a light touch upon her head, so she looked up into the wrinkled, ancient eyes of the Clan Mother, who now was lifting one of her golden braids and feeling it with both hands. Gunda began to laugh again, and the old woman gently lay it back upon Gunda's chest.

"I have never seen anything like this hair…" she told Anask'ala, adding, "It shines like the sun. Surely the Great Mother must love the girls of this odd-looking clan." She patted Gunda's head, then looking directly at Anson, asked him why they had come, putting both of her palms up to her sides with an exaggerated shrug. She stared at him for some time, and suddenly, he seemed to brighten, and nodded, then swiveled around, pointing back from where they'd come. The Clan Mother nodded. He must be telling me where they came from, she thought, wondering how to illustrate her next question, but he stood up suddenly, pointing to his chest, then counting upon both hands, curling each finger back as it was counted, once, twice, three, no four full hands. He raised both his hands overhead, then pointed back again.

Watching the entire series of gestures, Anas'kala asked her grandmother, "Does he mean to say there are four hands more of them coming? Is that what he is saying?"

"Yes, possibly, but why would he want us to know that?" The old woman's brows drew down as she pondered the answer. Anson again knelt and spoke to them, saying, "I don't know if you understand me, but maybe I can explain again." He waited until the old woman nodded and then rose slowly again, this time, stepping back two steps, then again counting out four hands, then he struck a pose with a hand clenched over his shoulder as if throwing a spear. He lunged towards the two women, who shrank back. Suddenly, the young man who had been so agitated lunged free of his comrades grip, and ran at Anson, his fists raised, yelling and screaming at him.

Anas'kala saw Mokolo lunge and saw him come running. She quickly stood, and put her hands out towards him, screaming, "Stop! Stop! Come no further! These people are beloved of the Great Mother, and no harm can come to them!"

"But... but they... they killed my father! I must kill them!" Mokolo cried out in anguish, but he stopped, just behind the Clan Mother, who now had turned slowly, glaring at him and raising her fist. He collapsed in a heap, crying out his error and asking forgiveness.

"Of course, father of my daughter's children to be. You are confused. We don't know these people, but I tell you to show them respect. They have come with news from the Great Mother herself, and we must treat them well. Do you understand, Mokolo?" She saw his tears, knew his sadness and anger.

"Yes, yes, Mother, I understand. It is hard for me, though, to ... to treat them as our own. They are not our own, they are... other men, come to take our home from us. Is that not so?" He cringed as he spoke the words. The Mother had used his name. It struck fear into his heart and now he was showing Anask'ala a part of him he was not proud of.

"Yes, Mokolo. You are right. They will come and they will force us to leave as we always have, but not these two. Do you see that? They are trying to speak with us. The man is a mighty hunter. He carries death in his hands, yet he lays it on the ground. You must do the same."

"Yes, Mother. I will try."

Seeing her future husband's fear and pain, Anask'ala rose and joined him, kneeling behind the Clan Mother. She reached out, and smoothed his eyebrows, and touched her finger to his lips. It seemed to soothe him. She hoped she could be forgiven for the showing of affection in daylight with the whole clan there to see.

Anson exhaled, having in his mind, narrowly avoided being beaten to death by a very angry young…man. He saw that his motions might have been seen as a threat, and understood. *The old woman means everything to these people. I must make her understand that only death follows behind me.* He again slowly stood, and went through the motions twice more, until suddenly, the younger woman's eyes grew round and she spoke to the older woman, very quickly and with alarm.

"Mother! He has come to … to warn us! There are more coming who mean to … hunt us, to attack us!"

Looking up at her granddaughter, the Clan Mother nodded, then replied, "It is just as I saw in my dream. They come soon, but this man has risked the anger of his fellows by coming to warn us. I will return… now to my bed, but I want you to bring this man and his daughter with you, into the cave and give them food and water before you tell the whole clan what you just told me. I had hoped we might have waited until after the winter, but the time to follow the path to the endless water has come. You must tell them." She tottered, trying to rise. Anask'ala steadied her from behind, then helped her stand fully. She made motion for Anson and Gunda and her poor, stricken husband to be, to follow her back to join the rest of the clan.

As the small group moved slowly into the cave, The Clan Mother leaned heavily upon both Anask'ala and Mokolo's arms. Anask'ala called out the Clan Mother's words to everyone. Hearing them, the old Food Mother ran back to prepare a small meal for their guests while the Fire Master's helpers added fuel to the fire to warm the cave as the light began to fade. Datolo found Anson's weapons, lying upon the ground, forgotten in the excitement. He took them up in his arms, and followed behind as the other man and his daughter were led inside.

Several deerskins had been laid upon the floor of the cave, near the fire-pit, and Anask'ala motioned for Anson and Gunda to sit upon them. She pointed to the Clan Mother, then to the darkness yawning in the back of the cave. Anson nodded, understanding that the old woman must rest. Once he was seated atop the soft skins he felt Gunda climb into his lap, and he embraced her, saying, "I think everything will be alright now." He thought for a moment, wondering how he could make Gunda understand, but added, "I needed you to be with me, Do you understand?"

"Of course, father! Why do you think I kept smiling and laughing? I didn't think it would work as good if *you* did that." She snuggled against his chest, and he dropped his chin to her head. Maybe, he thought, it had been the right thing to do after all. As Anson watched the flames, Datolo approached and laid his hand upon Anson's shoulder, then looking into his eyes, gently placed Anson's weapons next to him on the cave floor. He smiled, and spoke a few words which meant nothing to Anson.

"You will eat and rest. You will be safe here with us."

Anson saw the gentleness in the man's eyes, and nodded and smiled in reply as the Food Mother brought out a meal of meat and acorn cakes and berries. Gunda recognized the food, it wasn't all that different from what they ate in the village, and she said, excitedly, "Thank you! I'm very hungry and my father is, too!"

"Gunda, wait. Let all the serving be finished before you begin, to show respect to the women who have prepared this food for us."

"Yes, father." Her voice betrayed her disappointment, but she licked her fingers, where she'd touched the steaming meat. The work of preparation went on as they watched. Anson noticed he was the only man sitting nearby. The rest waited off to the side. He also saw the other men didn't even really watch what was being done to bring the meal together. How very odd, he thought. His own stomach was beginning to growl as the cooking smells engulfed him.

# # # #

"There. The trolls' lair lies above, in that far cave." Kells whispered to Nils and pointed out the dark mark on the far cliff wall. Kells' eyes shone brightly even in the semi-darkness of early morning. Nils considered the distance, and that some may be about to shout an alarm if the hunting party were seen. He motioned to the remaining party of hunters, pointing at a nearby deadfall whose roots blocked out the view from the trolls' cave. They all soon were huddling in its shadow.

Kells' excitement was making him shake slightly. Nils felt it through his arm, so he lay his hand upon Kells shoulder and said, quietly, "We must wait until the darkness falls, to climb up to a better position to watch them. We must remain hidden, so that we will know how best to kill them, once we have watched."

Kells nodded, but never took his eyes from the cave mouth. It was too far to see any activity around it clearly, but he would watch and see what he could. Nils left him and returned to the rest, gathered in the shadows near the deadfall in the shelter of its huge root mass. All were alert, their weapons ready, but Nils waved his hands horizontally in front of himself, and they relaxed. He gathered them around himself and in hushed tones, told them the plan, then selected two of them to scout ahead, slowly and quietly, to find several possible vantage points that would allow a view into the cave.

After they left, creeping up the wooded slope towards the ridge crest, he returned to his kit and rested. The sun crept up higher in the sky, sending its warmth into the valley. Nils pulled at his wet deerskin shirt. It had rained almost the entire night, and everyone was soaked, but they were still ready for whatever came. The warming sun began to force the ground near the creek to give up its moisture and a haze rose from the tall reeds and grasses. *It might become fog.* He hoped it would. Fog might serve his plan, He could send a second party to skirt around to the far side, hidden in the fog. Only time would tell him how to proceed. He checked his knife's edges, and counted his arrows.

\# \# \# \#

Anson watched Gunda, now sitting in a ring of other children. All girls, no boys. He saw boy children, but they kept to themselves. Gunda was laughing as each of the other girls would roll a bundle of fur and skin to her in turn. She rolled it to the next. It made him smile, seeing a game between children where no words were shared. Children, he thought, can be open to games.

Not grown men, though. They must do hard things. Only in that way can the children have their games. He thought of his wife and of his other children waiting for him to return. He hoped they were not sad, but he knew they probably were, and afraid, too. What he and Gunda were doing was a very hard thing, but it was very important. He even wondered if the two kinds of people might not become friends and share things with each other. He already had seen the ways of their healing. *Better ways*, he thought.

Mokolo and Anask'ala lay together on the huge bearskin bed prepared for them. Both were breathless and both smiled as they looked into each other's eyes. Mokolo was sure that the Great Mother must love them very much to have made bringing life so… full of pleasure. He stroked Anask'ala's side, from the curve of her breast,

192

down to her hip. Just feeling the touch of her skin seemed to kindle a fire in his heart, as well as his man-spear. She snuggled closer to him, then whispered, thinking of the other man and his little girl.

"They are so odd, so thin looking… like they don't get enough to eat. I almost feel sorry for them. The girl is happy enough, and her hair shines like the sun, but… they don't seem like us at all."

"Just as I thought. I don't fear them. I do wonder what they are thinking as I can't tell from their eyes. Their eyes look like water!"

Anask'ala giggled as he stroked her again, then whispered, "They look like they could be carried off by a strong gust of wind!" They giggled together and soon slept again. As night began to fall outside, she woke suddenly. Something inside felt different. She put her hand down on her belly, and wondered if she had new life inside of her. There had been more than enough seed, she knew. She rose quietly, leaving Mokolo to sleep and crept back, amidst the sleeping forms of women and children, to where she saw a soft glow of light coming from the entrance to the Clan Mother's place.

She knelt and called softly, "Mother? Mother? Are you awake?"

"Yes… Yes, child, come to me." When Anask'ala knelt at her bedside, she asked, "Is there something troubling you?"

"No… yes. Does new life feel special. You know, inside?" Anask'ala held her belly with both hands and leaned over towards her grandmother, expectantly

"Well… it may. Or it may not, child, it's different for every woman. I knew when I felt your mother begin her life in my belly." She tried to focus her weary eyes on her granddaughter's face, then saw how she was holding herself. "So," she said, "you and Mokotolo have made new life?"

"Yes, I feel... different. When I woke, just a moment ago, I felt all... unbalanced – almost like falling."

"Then it is yes. That was how it felt for me and for your mother as well. I'm proud of you. Mokolo gave you pleasure, too?" She lay her withered hand upon her granddaughter's hand. It felt almost hot to the touch. *Another sign*, she thought as she waited for the answer.

Anask'ala looked away for a moment, then turning back, replied, "Not at first. It hurt, just as you said, and it was over very quickly, but now... now it gives me so much pleasure I don't want to stop. Is that proper, Mother?"

"Of course, child, the Great Mother loves us and this is one of her most pleasurable gifts. How does it make you feel about your man?"

"It makes me feel I never want him to leave my bed... and I feel happy when he touches me. He smiles all the time. But, Mother... I worry about him. He still misses his father so deeply."

"He will always miss his father. We can't put away how we feel towards those of our clan that have gone. He is strong, and he makes you happy. Soon the new life will come, and both of you will begin your own new lives in a new home."

Anask'ala knew this would have to be discussed. When the sun came up, this was the day chosen, for her to lead the last group of the clan away towards the sun. She had put her worries away for the few hours she had with Mokolo, but now, she recounted all the preparations that had been completed. Only one remained. The last sacred bundle had to be withdrawn from the Mother Place so she could carry it with the clan, to their new home. It was sad, but it was also exciting. She had never been anywhere besides the valleys nearby and she longed for seeing her new home for the first time. Soon, she and Mokolo would follow the path up and over the ridge, and join with the rest of the clan waiting for them at the appointed spot.

She touched her grandmother's hand and asked her once again, "You still are determined to remain here? The men have prepared a carrying litter for you. We can bring you with us."

The answer was the same, "No child. This is where I shall stay. My time will soon be over and yours is just beginning. There is no other way. If I were stronger, I would have left in the Spring, myself. Now you carry the Clan for me." She coughed, then spat, and Anask'ala knew she was right. Her eyes filled with tears, and she reached to embrace the ancient healer, her own grandmother... the only living link to her own mother.

Deeply inhaling the smell of her skin and her hair, she said, "Thank you for teaching me. Thank you for being so wise and for loving us all!"

The old woman replied, stroking Anask'ala's back, "No, thank *you* child, for giving me *your* love and keeping my spirit alive for the clan. Thank *you*." They remained together the rest of the night, until the soft light of a new day crept around the passage into the inner cave.

# # # #

Nils smelled the smoke and an odor like cooking. The wind had changed, and now a breeze blew the smoke from the fire inside the cave right into his eyes. He wiped them, trying to get a better look. He and his half of the hunting party were perched out over the valley on an outcropping of rock. They all lay still, while Nils and two other men watched the activity in the cave below. There were few trolls. Mostly old women, from what he could see. When the breeze died, he could smell them, too. He wrinkled up his nose and wondered what foul things trolls must eat. He thought of Anson, and then the stories. "Ugghh!" he grunted aloud, hoping he didn't know what meat was burning down inside the cave.

Between the high ground where his party now hid and the trolls' lair, was a deep, dark cleft in the ridge line. It would make direct access to the cave very difficult, but the selected point had a very good view into the cave's mouth. A few troll children could just be seen through the smoke, and there were two or three taller trolls with spears to the left and right of the cave's mouth. *Sentries*, he thought. He knew that from where they lay hid, they could put arrows into most of the trolls easily. But he wanted to wait for the rest of the hunting party on the other side of the cave, to make sign that they had reached a safe hidden spot on the other side of the cave. The fog had hidden their movements, but it also hid them from Nils. Their part of the plan was to kill any trolls that tried to escape back down the path. The Seer words echoed in his memory. *All must be dead. Make sure of that, if you can.* He watched for a single arrow shot into the trees above the cave's mouth to alert him that it was time.

Nils' attention was drawn back to the cave mouth as a commotion broke through the smoke. Three trolls carried a small deer – a fawn -- to the descending pathway on a pole. While one held it down, the other two untied the lashings that held its legs to the pole. They began singing or croaking something to it in their nasty language, and it rose and shook itself off, then looking both ways, darted off down the path towards the valley floor. The singing sound continued, and grew louder as voices from within the cave began to join them. Trolls emerged, all carrying some kind of bundles, a few were dragging poles with burdens tied to them. They all began coming closer, then turning towards the ridge and disappeared, one after the other, behind a jutting section of the cliff face! He realized they were getting away, up a secret path or trail that couldn't be seen from where Nils and his hunters lay

watching. The sound of the singing or chanting grew
slowly louder, as the trolls climbed out of sight. He
shouted for his men to come to the edge.

Without waiting for the distant signal arrow, he
pointed to the last few, including a hugely fat, old one,
shuffling with a shorter troll who had a burden upon his
back and weapons in his hands. Nils nocked his first
arrow, and several other men joined him. He let it fly, off
towards the place where the last ancient troll disappeared
behind the jutting rock face. When he heard a scream, he
knew someone's arrow had found its mark. By this time,
all were ready to loose more arrows, and a second volley
flew up and down into the trees. Several more screams
were heard, then shouts. Nils motioned for his hunters to
fire more arrows, and they did. More screams were heard.

He then motioned for them to wait and keep their
remaining arrows for the attack he expected. He knew the
trolls had weapons, and expected them to be upon them in
moments, but as he waited, battle-prepared and tense, no
attack came. The only sounds were some distant shouts
and groans. He heard some whimpering as well, so he
knew their arrows had been true and deadly. He
congratulated his hunters with a smile.

As they clapped their chests and began talking of the
fight, Nils heard his name called from down at the cave.
He turned back to see Kells and the rest of the hunting
party climbing up over the rocky edge and assembling at
the mouth of the cave. He waved his bow over his head
twice, and Kells nodded. He saw Kells tap two hunters on
the back, and knew he was sending them into the cave's
darkness to flush out any remaining trolls in the shadows.
The two began shouting and calling back and forth as they
disappeared into the cave. Their voices at first, grew
fainter and fainter, then began to grow louder. Nils knew
they had gone deeply into the darkness before returning,

but they must bring torches to light the way and make sure all were gone.

Nils motioned his own hunters together and explained that they would now return the way they had come and join their fellows at the cave, so that they could make absolutely sure there were no trolls remaining inside. Young or old, all must be gone. He knew this must be done or they would never be safe again. Never. The Seer had spoken and they had done the deed. Nils was glad. None of the village children would ever need to fear trolls again. He turned and with a flourish of his arm, led them back down the slope towards the game trail to finish the work. He began thinking of the songs that would be sung about this day. He wanted to remember every detail and tell the Seer, so the Seer could weave it into a hero's tale for all the generations to come. Nils especially wanted to remember the hideous, ancient troll who had come last. He shivered thinking of her face as she had looked up, meeting his eyes.

Chapter 38

Anask'ala held her grandmother up against her chest. She cried, quietly and tried not to look at the small spear shaft that had entered the Clan Mother's neck and killed her as she tried to hide. A rough flow of blood had dried upon the old woman's lips and ran into the wrinkles, forming an ugly, dark red spiderweb. The small spears had rained down upon them suddenly. Two other clan men had been struck, but none killed. Mokolo had pulled one of the spears from his arm, and had just bound it up in deerskin and turned again to help raise the last of their belongings over the rock face to the ridge crest.

Mokolo felt tears on his cheeks. It had all happened so fast, he had no time to think. Anask'ala was right. The other man and his little daughter had come to warn them. Not to hurt them. Why would they do that? It was a question he would wonder for the rest of his life.

Two of the men waited nearby to help her with the Clan Mother's lifeless body. They all had to move quickly. They had all expected her to tell them what to do, but she was so shocked and terrified, that at first, she just told them all to run up the path, away from the arrows. When they stopped, no attack had followed, so seeing her grandmother had been killed, she asked two men to stay with her and help bury the Clan Mother quickly. They were all worried they would not have enough time to get everyone else to safety, but the burial must not be forgotten. At least she could give her grandmother that respect. Even if she had not had time to retrieve the sacred bundle.

They had been leaving, singing the leaving song, and Anask'ala told the Clan Mother she would bring her back to her bed before she retrieved the sacred bundle. "You should give your blessing to the last of the Clan as they climb up to leave, then we can return. It will give the clan strength and help them to say good bye to you." The Clan Mother agreed, so they had walked out at the end of the line, along with the other man and his daughter. The child had climbed up into a pack upon his back, and was trying to sing along with them when the first small spears fell.

She watched two clan-brothers claw at the small spears that had struck them and realized that the sacred bundle would have to remain where it was. The hopeless feeling that came with the realization rocked her. The life of the clan for countless generations. Now lost to them. She hoped she could find a woman who was also a maker, who could help her re-make it once they found their new home. She began thinking that maybe this was best. It should be the stone of their new home, just as the bundle left was the stone of their old home.

One of the men stripped some pine boughs down from the small trees along the path while the other one began to dig a shallow pit behind a rock outcrop with a slab of wood. The bottom of this gorge was soft, and full of runoff dirt, so the digging was fast and easier than they had expected. Soon both approached Anask'ala, asking, "Mother, we must take her if we are to escape. Now, Mother."

They had called her *Mother*. She touched her belly, thinking of the new life it held. Wiping her tears, she leaned back away, saying the words. "Go now, Mother, go to your peace. Guide us with your spirit and live forever in the life of the Clan you have carried in your heart." She began singing the death song quietly. She was filled with shame that she had not been able to lead a feast in the memory of her grandmother, but thought, *maybe when we're safe, in a new home, I will do that for her.*

Anask'ala stood, her knees barely able to hold her, and watched as they carried the Mother's body to the hole, now lined with pine boughs. They gently lowered her into the earth, covered her with more boughs and began covering her up with the dirt they'd dug from the hole, then laid flat rocks on top to protect it from scavengers and… others. It was a rude grave, not the grave of a sacred Clan Mother.

She looked around them, in the shadows of the deep gorge, and her eye fell upon what might have been a spot where the sun sent beams shining into the darkness. But that wasn't what it was. Mokolo stood nearby, in the shadows. His hand was to his face and she saw his body shaking. He is crying, she thought, and moved closer. Then she saw what had so disturbed Mokolo.

Curled together, behind a large tree and up against a rock, the other man and his golden haired daughter had breathed their last. She approached, singing quietly and thinking a prayer to the Great Mother: *This man was unknown as was his daughter, yet they were good, and brave. Please fold them into your heart and give their spirits peace…*

The shafts of several small spears cruelly protruded from the man's neck and his daughter, Anask'ala saw, had been struck twice in her back. There was blood everywhere, and drag marks telling her that they had lived for a moment, in the frenzy, and he had tried to crawl to safety while his heart was still beating. The soft golden hair fell along the girl's back to where the spears jutted from her now blood soaked deerskin shirt. Her hair was turning red with the blood as it ran to the ground. The other man's eyes were open, and he almost seemed to be asking some question, his mouth agape.

Anask'ala hurried to where the men were laying heavy stones atop the Clan Mother's grave, and said, "There are two more here that must be set to rest."

One of the men, turned to look, wondering who they had lost just as Mokolo approached. He saw the grave, and embraced Anasak'ala. "Come, he said, "let's join the rest. They are waiting ahead."

"No. Not yet. There are two more to bury." She pointed to the other man and his daughter's bodies.

"But they are not of the Clan, why do we show them honor? Time is short!"

"Today, I say that they... *are* Clan. They were good, brave people, and deserve to lie in honorable graves, not just prey of the carrion birds, foxes and wolves!" She took Mokolo by the hand and led him back into the shadows. In a few moments, they returned to where the Clan Mother lay. Anask'ala carried the lifeless young girl while Mokolo dragged her father over. The other two had been digging and soon, were bringing back pine boughs. Anask'ala reached into her bag which was on a strap across her shoulder. Once the sunshine haired girl was laid down atop her father's body, she sprinkled them both with dried, red flowers. The healing flowers. The other man's weapons were placed with him and his daughter with great respect. The long stick with the string was laid there gently. Mokolo looked down at it and his father's face came to him in his memory. He felt a tear run down his cheek.

Anask'ala knelt down and in a whisper, said, "I never knew your names, or what you came to tell us, but I know that you tried to help us... and I am grateful. Our Clan is grateful. I wanted to... to help you, and did, for a while at least. Go now, to your own peace and rest, and I will tell your story to all, that they may know that among our ancient enemies, the other men, are spirits of those who bear us no ill wishes." She stood, with Mokolo's help and together they quietly sang the death song until the two were covered deeply in the earth and large stones laid atop them.

Mokolo and the two remaining men nodded, and Mokolo said simply, "It's time to find our way to the rest of the Clan." Anask'ala wiped away her tears, and replied, "Yes, it *is* time." As they ran up the path, they heard far-off, ugly shouts coming from behind them; but soon, they had climbed up over the ridge and down the other side, and no one followed to pursue them or throw the small spears.

Mokolo was sore and tired, and his arm throbbed painfully. The bleeding had stopped at least. Anask'ala was panting as they ran, trying to catch her breath as were the other men, but they dared not stop. After the sun slowly passed overhead,   Mokolo saw the light filtering through the trees, grow brighter. Ahead, in a clearing, the rest of the Clan awaited them. Their new Clan Mother had shown how brave she was, and when the first child saw them coming from the edge of the woods, she raised both hands over her head and began to sing. The four burst from the edge of the woods with weary, smiling faces.

# # # #

" I don't understand," said Ariel Connor as she listened to the excavation assistant explain what they'd found above the burial in the stone gorge above the cave. "This makes no sense. You're telling me that you have another burial of modern humans interred alongside a Neanderthal female? Is that right?" She called to her associate, "Jens, did you see this yourself?"

He stumbled off the ledge he'd been climbing down from and caught his breath before replying, "Yes, that's it exactly. But there's more to it – there are two modern skeletons, entwined."

She shook her head. It was so far outside their experience, she couldn't grasp it.

Jens continued, "Yes, a male of medium height, along with the skeleton of a small female, probably a child. The smaller skeleton is curled up under the ribcage of the larger, covered by the arm long-bones. Nearby, is a traditional Neanderthal burial of a very old female, showing advanced joint degeneration and spinal curvature. Some bone beads and the remnants of evergreen boughs are there too."

He stepped over to his colleague, touching her shoulder. Ariel looked up, her face swimming with confusion and disbelief. "Are you sure they were all interred at the same time?"

"Yes. The soil has such a high clay component, such distinctive layering, that it is conclusive as far as I can see. Of course, you must see it for yourself." He added, "...and there is more to it. All three skeletons carry the signs of death involving the same projectile points as the first burials, down below the ledge. There are several protruding from the neck and spine of the Neaderthal female as well as the moderns. The young female had two in her spine. We've left them all in situ for the photographer and for your attention. Do you want to go right up?"

An hour later, Ariel crouched down in the excavated trench next to the joined modern skeletons. In her palm, she held two finely flaked points removed from what would have been the body cavities of the two. Near them, so close they might have been actually almost touching, lay the burial of the Neanderthal female, also clearly the victim of the same ancient murderers.

"Jens? What do these points say to you regarding who killed these people?"

"I was waiting for you to ask me that." He rejoined her from where he had been standing at the feet of the Neanderthal burial. "These points are not late Neanderthal points. They are probably the work of modern humans. I can tell from the delicacy of the notching at each base. It's much more refined than Neanderthal knapping, and from their size, they were arrow points."

"I know your theory regarding the bow versus the spear-thrower. It fits," she replied.

"It all fits together almost as if the Neanderthalers and these two modern humans were the casualties of some kind of ancient warfare, or a vendetta killing. What really surprises me is who buried these three? From the associated objects near the Neanderthal female, I would say it was Neanderthalers, yet here are two modern skeletons, laid with obvious care, in the same burial."

"This is not going to be an easy one to solve. I'm a little worried about where my mind is leading me here." Ariel wiped her forehead where a gnat had just landed. "I don't want anything disturbed further. Cover it all, and re-bury them once all the photography is finished. Is there enough light down here for good contrast?"

Jens replied, "Just barely, but it will do."

"Let's discuss this before you write your report up, OK? I want us to be on the same page when we have to explain our conclusions. The whole team will have to keep this to themselves, agreed?"

"Agreed, Ariel, but I think we already know where we're going to take this. It's ground you already covered, or tried to, a few years ago, right? It's going to upset all the applecarts, isn't it?"

"Yes. Apples are gonna roll everywhere if we do the right job. This may be a big one."

"I hope it is", said Jens, "a shake-up is long overdue!"

The End

Acknowledgements:

I have always had an appreciation for history's lessons since my eighth grade Western Civilization teacher, William Morrissette, back in Springfield, Oregon, told me about Walter M. Miller's novel A Canticle for Leibowitz. It took me years before I read it finally and understood what he meant. Bill also gave me an enjoyment for research and seeing how, as a species, we just never really learn from the past. I also want to thank my wife for her forbearance and insight and my editor, Wendy Bertsch of Ocean Highway Books, who believed in this story and helped me make it fit for readers.

The Author:

Richard Sutton has been called a storyteller and it suits him, as he's spent his life traveling from one tale to the next. He lives with his wife of many years and their three cats, above Long Island Sound. For more information visit his website/blog at www.sailletales.com